Two Lefts, One Right

TURNS IN LOVE SERIES: BOOK ONE

THE WRONG TURNS IN LOVE

RENÉE A. MOSES

GUSSYFLO PUBLISHING

This book is dedicated to my great-grandmother, Gustavia AKA Myne. You are now my angel, but you passed the love of writing down to me. I am doing this for the both of us.
To my mom, Florence AKA Bonnie, you knew I was a writer long before it ever crossed my mind. Thank you for believing in me and reading all my stories over the years. I am finally doing it. You've been waiting for me to take it seriously for years and I am glad I listened to you. I love you.

To my three babies, thanks for your patience. I've had many long nights to produce this book and many others. I promise it will pay off. I love you always.

To you, the reader, thank you for your support and most of all, Stay Blessed! Put God first and good things will come. Jesus saved and loves all of us, don't forget it.

Kim

My mom had finally called me back, but before I could answer it, my boss summoned me to her office. Mrs. Roland's timing couldn't be worse. It was the third day in a row that I'd been ignored by my family. We had one disagreement and Mom was getting back to me after multiple attempts to reach her. Maybe it was bigger than I thought.

My grandparents also let me know how disappointed they were in me to decide to shack up before marriage. It was going to happen eventually, so why not get the hard part out of the way?

The closer I got to thirty with no name change, the more I felt like a damn kid. Nothing I did was good enough because I was the last to do it. Being a middle child and the only unmarried one was a tough place in my family.

I'd been with my boyfriend for so long that it felt like we were married except for one aspect: we didn't live together. So, we chose to take that step against my family's admonition.

Even my baby sister warned me not to go through with it until we were married. My whole thing was that if we couldn't live together now, how the hell would we be able to do it then.

I'd like to test it out before I'm officially stuck in the same house with someone forever.

Once we were married, that would be it. My family would damn near disown me if I divorced my husband for anything other than a life-threatening, domestic violence situation. Otherwise, I'd be expected to stick with him through anything. The only thing I'd been that loyal to was my career.

I went into Mrs. Roland's office and sat in the chair opposite her. She was a great boss and her advice regarding my personal life helped me through a lot, especially with my family. The previous morning, we discussed my decision to move in with my boyfriend and she heard me out.

For a woman with three adult children and a marriage that started over thirty years ago, she never let me down with the hard decisions. Mrs. Roland was on my side with this one and that was all I needed. At least one person whose opinion I trusted wasn't telling me that I was going to hell for testing the waters with my living situation.

After a few seconds of her finishing a phone call, she looked at me and smiled.

"Kim, I have an interesting opportunity that I want to offer you."

"Okay. What is it?" I asked.

Something in the way she said it made me nervous. "As you know, the company is expanding. I got the HR department set up in Louisiana some months ago, but the company is moving faster than I can. It took a little while to get everything together, but it was only one state over..." she paused, then squinted.

"What are you saying, Mrs. Roland?"

"Look, I wouldn't ask this of you if I had a better option. From the talk we had yesterday, I understand that you are all set to move soon. This could be considered perfect or horrible timing, but you are the only one I'd trust to go in my place."

If I wasn't confused before, I was now.

Mrs. Roland took a deep breath, then told me, "The next office to be opened is in Denver and I was asked to go and get the department set up there. Being that my husband hadn't been feeling well enough for me to leave him, I suggested that you take on this task."

I coughed violently. The air didn't come into my body correctly when she said *I* was leaving.

"Are you okay?" she asked.

"Yes, I'm sorry about that." I composed myself. "So, I have to move to Denver?"

"Temporarily. An apartment will be furnished and paid for. We'd communicate the same way we did when I left, and Linda was in charge here."

"Yeah, but this place was already established. Are you sure you want me to go? Why not send Linda?"

"Don't tell her I told you this, but she's about to be let go. It has something to do with her hiring a few people she knew personally that obviously weren't qualified to do their jobs. I should have checked everything out myself, but we'd been doing this for so long I thought I could trust her judgment," she whispered.

"Oh, wow."

"So, Kim, do you think this would be something you'd consider?" she asked.

"You know how much I love my job. I am a team player. Whatever you need, I'm here to get it done."

Her smile illuminated the room. "That's great to hear. I don't know why I was nervous to ask you about it. And I'm supposed to be the boss." She giggled.

"Do you know the time frame of all this? Like, when will I need to leave and how long it will take?" I inquired.

"You should be expected to leave in a couple of weeks at the least to start preparing some face-to-face interviews and contact some staffing agencies that we're connected to in Colorado. I have done some of the paperwork and we have a staffing plan ready. It's estimated to be about eight weeks."

"Say what now?"

Two months? Shit! She was right when she said it could be the worst timing. I didn't see it going that well after telling everyone this news.

"Will that be a problem?" she asked, genuinely concerned.

"No. Eight weeks is fine. I will make it work."

"Well, alright. I will let them know and I will get back to you with more details."

"Yes, ma'am. Thank you for thinking of me."

Linda walked right past the door when I stepped out of the office. Was she eavesdropping? Maybe she knew she'd been caught handing out jobs. I tried not to make any eye contact. If she approached me, she might see right through me.

My baby was out of town visiting his grandparents for the week. I didn't want to drop this bomb on him over the phone, but he wouldn't be coming home for a few days.

Honesty was the key to the door of good communication, as my dad would say. So, hopefully, if I told him immediately, he'd understand.

When he called me on my way home from work, we planned to video chat that night. I would tell him then. At least I'd be able to see him.

Before going home, I dropped by my parents' house. Since my mom called me earlier, I'd figured she was moving on about the shacking up thing. No one was home when I pulled up.

I needed something to do. Denise responded to my text to meet up and get a drink. Knowing how my dude was, tonight may be epically difficult.

A little venting and two margaritas later, I felt better about talking to him. Denise swore he'd be understanding, but she was naïve to the man I knew personally. Being reasonable was not his strong suit.

He seemed amazing to outsiders and sometimes he was. The other side of that coin was a man that I didn't want to be around. I prayed for the best and made the call.

ᛗᛗᛗ

ON FRIDAY, I GOT HOME FROM WORK AND SHOWERED before dressing for dinner at McCormick & Schlick's. My ride blew the horn and we headed to the restaurant in silence.

Brian had to be the sweetest man on the planet. He planned a beautiful three-year anniversary surprise vacation to Hawaii. Now we're at this fancy restaurant.

We met in college almost ten years ago. We were lab partners in our chemistry class at the University of Houston. He turned out to be a true, perfect catch.

It was time for the toast. Brian got everyone's attention while staying seated.

"I can't believe three years passed by as fast as they did," he said, then looked at me.

"Kim, I don't know how you knew, but I'm glad you introduced me to the most beautiful woman God ever created. No offense. You cool, but my honey is above all."

Everyone chuckled. I scrunched my face at the both of them.

"Denise, you are and always will be the love of my life and I will celebrate the day we said 'I do' forever. You truly saved me. I was only a youngin' hanging with lowlifes and had no hope for the future."

Brian looked at Trent and so did everybody else.

"Screw you," Trent countered. "Just get on with it and stop taking digs at me and my lady."

Trent put his arm around me and kissed the side of my

head. The two of them were like brothers. Brian hooked us up back in college. The four of us have grown up so much since then.

Denise and Brian were what I wanted to be like when the time came. There was a rock on my hand, but it had only been three months since Trent proposed.

"I know. Is this toast about me or them?" Denise joked.

"He must have had too many glasses of water," I said.

The whole group laughed, especially at the look Brian gave me. He doesn't drink alcohol of any kind. I only saw him drink once back in college and it was a rough night. It made him vow to never touch liquor again. While it was admirable, I couldn't do it.

After he finished what he had to say, Denise gave a very brief speech. It was a beautiful thing to see them like this. In a couple years, we should be celebrating our wedding anniversary as well.

The dinner came to an end and the happy couple's family left. Trent had this bright idea to go to a club, of all places, to finish the night off. I had no idea why they even agreed to it.

I was not in the mood. There was so much on my mind and we still haven't finished packing our places up. The dinner should have been enough.

As we walked out, Denise grabbed my arm and we moved away from the guys a bit.

"So, how did Trent take the news?" she asked. "He didn't."

"Kim?" she whined. "You are about to marry this man. You cannot be keeping secrets from him. Especially one as big as this."

"Look, I know I should have told him by now, but he's been in a funk. I didn't want to make it worse."

"It will undoubtedly be worse if you don't say something before your butt is on a plane."

"You know I wouldn't do that. We will talk about it soon enough. Trust me," I told her. "Mmhmm."

I turned back to make sure the men weren't in earshot. They were still near the restaurant entrance.

"Why the hell do we have to go to a club for a wedding anniversary? That makes no sense to me. Even if you wanted to, why the hell do I have to?" I complained.

"I thought it was weird, too. Brian said Trent wanted to take us out. I don't care either way," she said.

"Ugh, I don't know why his dumbass chose a club. He knows how much I hate clubs. Someone always grabs my ass and I can't ever identify the creep. There's usually a group of them when it happens to me. I hate it."

"Yeah and if you tell your daddy over there, he might start a brawl. 'Nobody better touch my woman,'" Denise joked, doing her Trent impression.

"Girl, don't get me started on his overprotective ass. Anyway, I need you to get me out of this. Go tell them you don't feel good or something."

"Damn, you don't want to hang out with me that bad?" She pouted.

"Don't do that. It has nothing to do with you and you know it."

We glanced over at the men. They were having what looked like a deep conversation. Then again, it was probably about sports.

"Fine. I will do it...for you."

"Thank you. Besides, you need to go home and be with your man. Keep the party going in the bedroom."

"You nasty."

"Girl, you are married. You better go do what married people get to do with no guilt."

"Yeah, right. Like your ass ever felt guilty about doing your thang."

"Well, not during." We laughed a little too loud.

I guess the guys were done talking since they walked over to us. Both of them gave the valet dude our tickets.

Brian hugged his wife, looking down at her. He was tall and slightly buff. The guys used to workout faithfully back in the day and both still had the muscles from then. Trent was bigger than Brian in build, but a few inches shorter.

Brian was always cleanly shaven. We used to tease him that he had no choice since his facial hair never quite grew in. Trent could grow a full beard in what felt like a week. It made him look rough at times, but I loved it on him.

Trent took his appearance very serious. He only bought high-end name brands as if everyone would judge him if he wore anything else. It was his style that initially attracted me to him. Brian, on the other hand, had no defined style. He usually threw on a t- shirt and jeans. He was simple like that.

Denise and Brian were so cute together. She was taller than me. It was like we were the short couple compared to them. Trent was a decent height, but my five-three frame brought down our average height as a couple.

"Brian, do you think we can skip the club tonight? I'm not feeling too good." Denise conjured up some baby voice.

"Of course, beautiful."

"Aww, what's the matter?" I asked.

She looked at me like I was crazy and shook her head. "Um, I'm not sure. I don't feel right."

"That's too bad, Denise. I hope you feel better," I told her.

We hugged. "Something is really wrong with you," she whispered in my ear.

I also gave Brian a hug before we headed to our cars. Once we were on the road, Trent made turns that weren't taking me home.

"Where are we going?" I asked.

"I thought we were still going out," he said.

"Why would we? You clearly don't care about what I want, but I'd rather go home. Thank you."

"Whatever," he said with too much attitude.

"Whatever to you." I stared out the passenger window.

"Grow up, Kimberly."

"Fuck you, Trenton."

I heard him take a deep breath. If he knew better, that would be the end of the conversation. It was.

I didn't want to fight any more than we already had. We met our quota for the week. Like a fool, I thought Trent would be supportive of this opportunity for me to show what I can handle at work. That's a lie, I expected him to be upset but not be so vocal about it. He could have faked it a bit. It was a typical Trent reaction: selfish and demanding.

We hadn't talked to each other for days. He picked me up for the dinner party because he loved to put on a good act for everyone. Outsiders thought that we were a great couple and had the best relationship. Nothing or no one was perfect, but he wanted the assumption to be made that he was.

Denise knew much of what we'd gone through and so did Brian. He was a good friend to the both of us and a secret mediator. I would tell him things and ask him to talk to Trent about it from a man's point of view.

My man was extremely stubborn, and I usually got through to him by way of Brian. It was my best bet to get my point across and worked for the most part.

This time I was on my own. Denise didn't even know what this fool had been like since I told him about the tempo-rary move. The last thing I needed was for her to agree with him. She was rooting for us harder than we were. If this oppor-tunity would put a strain on our relationship, she'd annoy-ingly try to convince me to stay.

Being together for almost eight years was a huge factor in my decision to accept his proposal. It wasn't like I had many other options on the table. Plus, he made me happy most of the time. Those hiccups we had were in the past.

Trent cheated a few times when we first started dating and again about two years ago. We broke up for a few months the last time, but he fought enough to get me back. Once I somewhat trusted him again, I didn't throw it in his face. I forgave him, and we moved on. Even when he had his disrespectful streaks anytime he got angry, I forgave him.

I supported him through multiple career changes and his childish ways. All I needed was for my man to have my back and trust that this would make us stronger. If he couldn't do it now, then what type of marriage would we have? Definitely not one where the man dictates, and the woman acts accordingly. Not me. Any sane person who dealt with me should know by now that I bow down to no one but God.

When we pulled up to the apartments, I couldn't get out of the car fast enough. He drove to the entrance for me to scan my gate card. Instead, I exited the car and headed toward the gate near the office.

I'd rather walk all the way to the back of the complex in the dark than to spend another unnecessary moment with him. And we're supposed to move in together next week?

Minutes after I made it into my place, someone knocked on my door. "Kim, open up," Trent demanded from the other side.

"Go home. I don't want to talk to you."

"Babe, let me come in. I'm sorry for earlier. Please?"

Like a dumbass, I opened it. After I closed and locked the door, I stared at him.

I wanted to see if he was really sorry.

"So, now you are cool with me leaving?"

"Fuck no! I told you it's not a good time."

"You told me how you felt. But you cannot tell me what I can't do."

"Look, I am your man. Soon to be your husband. How does it look for you to up and leave when we are supposed to be planning a wedding?" he asked, getting loud.

"Negro, there will be no wedding if you don't stop talking to me like that. I don't understand why you are tripping so hard over a few weeks, Trent. You act like you don't trust me or something."

"I don't."

He walked to the kitchen and grabbed a bottle of water from my refrigerator. I came from behind him and snatched it out of his hand before he could open it.

"Get the hell out. I ain't got time for this bullshit. I'm tired and need to go to sleep."

"You already kicking me out?" he asked.

"Yeah, when dumb shit start falling out of your mouth, it's time to go."

"Dumb?"

"Oh, you didn't hear yourself? You don't trust me. The woman who never fucked or even looked at another man since I met you. The woman who took your stupid ass back after you fucked up. Now, I'm supposed to suffer and hold myself back in my career because of your insecurity? I don't think so."

He swiped his hand toward me and walked to my bedroom. There were boxes everywhere. He tripped and almost fell.

"That's what you get," I said.

Trent walked back toward me as if he would run me over. I wished he would.

"You need to get out of my face," I told him.

"Or what?"

"Don't play with me."

"No, you're the one who needs to stop playing. Tell the people at your job that you ain't going."

"Hell no."

"No? You asked me how I felt about it and I told you. You think you're still going?"

"First of all, you are not my daddy and I don't need your permission to do a goddamn thing. Second, I am going. End of discussion."

"No, it's not."

"Oh, but it is. I already accepted, and I will be leaving next weekend."

He looked like I insulted his mom or something. His eyes kept squinting as if he was cussing me out in his head.

"You ready to get out yet?" I asked.

Trent leaned against the refrigerator. "Hold up. You came to me with this shit last week like it wasn't for sure. Now, you're really going?"

"Like I said, it wasn't a question. I told you what the plan was and that I was going to go."

"Nah, you never said it was actually happening. You definitely didn't say you were supposed to go next week."

"Why would I? You fucking lost it when I barely mentioned it at first. I wasn't in the mood for Hurricane Trenton. So, I didn't tell you the whole plan."

He laughed, and it freaked me out. The calm before the storm was never easy to brace for.

"Trent, you need to leave."

"Why are we doing this?" he asked.

"Doing what? I'm trying to be the adult about this. I need my job, and this will be beneficial for me. You, on the other hand, are acting like it's the end of the world. I am doing what is best for our future."

"That's what you tell yourself to sleep at night."

"I sleep fine. I am not doing anything wrong."

He laughed. "You never do, huh?"

"Whatever."

"Yeah, whatever."

He walked toward the door. I refused to look his way. Trent loved slamming doors to let it be known that he was upset as if it was never obvious beforehand.

The door never closed. That fool left my front door wide open. I looked outside; no one was there. Childish.

After my shower, I figured his mom, Sheryl, would've called or texted. She was his go-to whenever he thought he was right. By the end of the conversation, she'd have both sides of the story and could make her own judgment. I wouldn't be surprised if she got on me about my decision. Whoever didn't like it would have to deal with it without me.

CHAPTER TWO

Kim

I SPENT ALL SUNDAY PACKING AND MAKING LISTS OF what I needed to do for the move. Ones for the rental home we were about to share and for the trip to Denver.

My dad called to check on me. He was the only one that worried whenever there was tension between me and my mom. I respected what he had to say, but I was about as hard-headed as he taught me to be.

My family knew about the job opportunity the day after I accepted it, but not too much was said. Daddy congratulated me over the phone that day. Maybe he felt it would postpone the move with Trent. I let him run with that for the time being.

Daddy invited me over for a dinner he had planned for the following night. I agreed to show up and asked for prayer that it didn't get out of hand.

After church service, I called Trent. Once again, he ignored me. It seemed like being ignored was the present theme of my life. I wished everyone else would grow up.

No one wanted to talk to me because they knew they couldn't change my mind about anything I was doing. My parents taught me to stand up for what I believed in. I guess they never thought what I wanted wouldn't match their plans for me.

The only person that I could be honest with was Trent's mom. Sheryl knew about everything even after the big argument on Friday. We talked briefly yesterday. She even apologized for her son behaving the way he did.

I loved his mom and his sisters. They were understanding even if they didn't agree with me. Trent must be like his absent father because the women in his life were sane.

Denise and I went out for brunch after we left church. I sort of broke away from going to church with my parents. My mom knew how to get under my skin so well that I couldn't even hear the preacher over her disappointment. It wasn't about anything professionally. In her eyes, I was a great example when it came to my work ethic and how I managed to move forward in my career.

My personal life was where we'd bump heads. She treated me like everyone would know everything I did that she didn't like and would shun her or something. My life was mine and mine alone, but she couldn't see it that way.

I finally told Denise the whole truth about how Trent took the news. For some reason, she was really shocked by the rift between us because of this.

Of course, she wanted us to win together, but she knew most of Trent's ways. It didn't surprise me as much as I wanted it to. Him being mature and understanding would be something worth gasping over.

The waiter at this little spot we found on Westheimer gave us our mimosas and took our food order.

"Well, I was hoping he'd be happy for you."

"Yeah, you and me both." I took a long sip of my drink and noticed Denise looking at me funny.

"What?"

"Promise me you won't be mad at me."

"Nope. Say what you gotta say."

"Kim, I love you and I do want you to be happy.
You know that."

"Mmhmm."

"Is this really worth it?"

I looked up at the ceiling. These people were about to force me into making this move permanent.

"Stop that. I'm only asking because you two have been through so much. Even in the last year. Your miscarriage, the proposal, moving in together, and now this. It may be too much excitement and disappointments for him. Maybe he wants to keep you close."

I made a face that I immediately regretted.

"What was that for?" she asked.

"Nothing."

"Tell me."

With a long inhale, I exhaled the words, "It's the pregnancy thing."

"What about it? It's been like four or so months, right? Is he still down about the baby?"

"I know I am going to sound like I'm an evil person but..."

"But what? Did you abort the—"

"No! I would never."

"Oh. Girl, my heart." She put her hand to her chest for a few moments.

"I kind of never told him about the baby."

"Kimberly Chanel Duncan. You've got to be freaking kidding me."

"Everything happened so fast and I didn't want to hurt him. I was initially keeping it from my family and didn't tell him. The baby was gone before I knew it. You were the only person who knew about it."

"I told Brian."

"What?" I damn near shouted.

"I didn't know it was a secret, secret."

"Dee, I told you not to say anything."

"But that's my husband. I couldn't keep it from him."

"Why the hell not? That was my business."

"You said Trent doesn't know."

"That seems impossible if Brian knew about it," I said, trying to think of the timeline of all this.

"True."

"Dammit. Maybe that's why he's so mad at me. He probably knew this whole time and that I didn't tell him myself. He's been over the top mad."

"Trent would have said something by now though, right?"

"I don't even know anymore."

"See, all of these secrets. They are never good in any relationship."

The food came but I couldn't even eat. If Trent was aware of our failed pregnancy and that I hid it from him, then that was it. The spiral we've been on since our engagement would make complete sense. I got a box for my food and told Denise that I needed to go home. She apologized to me about everything before I left.

I called Brian, but he didn't answer. He texted me that he was with Trent at my future mother-in-law's house. I told him it was urgent.

A few minutes later, he called me back. I asked if he ever talked to Trent about the miscarriage. He claimed he vaguely mentioned it before, but Trent acted like he didn't know what he was talking about. So, Brian dropped it. He thought Trent wanted to avoid the topic. Based on what he told me, I was in the clear.

The movers were scheduled to come in a couple days. I sat on the floor of my kitchen and ate my food from the restaurant. I watched reruns of *Living Single* on my tablet until my dad texted, asking me to bring some vanilla ice cream on the way over. I'd completely forgotten about dinner.

ʬʬʬ

MOM PREPARED A SMALL HAM WITH CORNBREAD dressing, corn, peas, and yams. This kind of food was why I always looked forward to Thanksgiving. Then it began to feel like a trap. If she was too upset to talk to me before, why was she doing this?

I greeted everyone. My older brother and little sister were there with their families. I was on my own. My sister-in-law usually had my back, but she couldn't stand a chance against Mom. I kept my mouth closed unless spoken to.

Mom said about two words to me in the first twenty minutes. I played with my nephews for a while. When dinner was ready, Dad forced me to sit next to Mom. He prayed over the food and added a request for everyone to be respectful and loving during the dinner. We'd soon see if God would grant that one.

After everyone dug in, I thanked my mom for all the food she had cooked. My sister, Keisha, mentioned that it included all my favorites.

"Well, your sister will be gone for the next two months. I wanted to make her a good meal before she left," Mom said.

"Thank you. I really appreciate it," I told her.

"You are so spoiled," my brother, Kendrick, joked.

"Shut up," I said.

"Where's Trent?" Tina, my sister-in-law, asked.

My mom's face twitched, and Tina's eyes widened before she quickly looked down at her plate.

"He couldn't make it," I answered.

"That's probably because he wasn't invited," Keisha mumbled loud enough for everyone to hear.

I had to laugh to myself. My family was crazy. They knew how Mom was and yet they kept going there.

"Why y'all gotta treat my future brother-in-law like that? I'm sure he would have loved to eat with us. He may not be invited near this house again after this week," Kendrick rubbed in.

He grinned until I kicked his leg under the table. "What? They not mad about you shacking up no more?" he asked.

"I hate you," I mouthed.

He winked at me.

Kendrick loved when I was at the center of attention. Well, at least negative attention. It would take Mom's wrath off of Tina. At times, I thought Tina would have snapped and left him. Our mom was pretty harsh and very controlling. Tina wasn't headstrong like the rest of us. She took it all to heart.

I didn't know why my brother acted so stupid right now. As soon as I'm gone, Mom would be back on Tina's case about every little thing.

"That's enough guys," Dad finally said.

"Sorry," Kendrick told him.

"Are you all packed up for Denver?" Mom asked with emphasis on Denver.

I guess it was not to be confused with concern about being packed up to go to hell in her mind.

"Yes, the whole place is packed."

"You're taking everything with you?" Kendrick asked with that dumb smirk.

If my parents weren't right here, I'd flip him the bird. "No, I am taking some clothes to Colorado. The rest is going to my new place with my fiancé, Trenton."

Mom got up and went into the kitchen. We all knew I should not have gone there, but she played it off by checking on the apple pie.

"I'm about two seconds to kicking all of y'all out? Why are you trying to upset your mother?" Dad said, looking at me.

"That's wasn't me, Daddy. Kendrick started it."

"Do you want me to finish it?" he asked all of us.

"No, sir," we all answered one after the other.

The rest of the evening was fake as hell. We pretended to be a happy family that got along great. As long as we didn't talk about the many elephants in the room, we were good.

We ate dessert and played a few games before I called it a night. Mom was being too weird, and I couldn't play along anymore. I gave everyone hugs and kisses except Kendrick. I punched him in the arm. Punk ass.

I missed Sheryl's call while I was there. I'd talk to her another time. I'd had enough for the day and wanted to go to bed as if none of it happened.

Trent

I turned my phone off after the second day of nonstop calling. Kim would have to live with her decision to leave me the way she did. Her boxes were everywhere, and they would stay everywhere. Unpacking my own shit was the only thing on my agenda. Maybe I should send her things to Colorado since that's where she wanted to be.

Brian kept texting me earlier, too. She had been calling him to get to me. I didn't get it. I told her not to go and she left anyway. Why the fuck did she care now?

Everyone thought Kim was so perfect and I was always the one in the wrong on every occasion. She even had my own mom on her side. No one understood me or ever tried to. All that mattered was Kim getting her way. Her family came before me and so did her job.

What was so hard and demanding about hiring people? She acted like she would run the company one day if she jumped at their every request. I expected more from a woman who claimed she wanted to spend the rest of her life with her man.

What kind of wife would she even be if she couldn't

compromise for my sake this one time? I hoped she'd feel bad enough to come home soon and tell her job to find somebody else. I didn't want to hear a damn thing from no one until Kim was back here where she belonged.

Someone knocked on my door. It must've been the pizza and wings I had ordered. When I opened it, I immediately wished I checked the peephole first.

"What's up, man?" Brian asked.

"Nothing. Whatchu want?"

"Can I tell you from the inside? It's hot out here."

The pizza man pulled up. I stepped outside and waited for him to bring my food. I paid him, then went back inside. The door was left open, but I didn't say shit. It was obvious Kim sent him here. They seemed to be tighter than we were.

"So, you gonna act like you don't see me?" Brian asked, still standing by the front door.

"I see you, nigga. I spoke to you, didn't I?"

The living room was between us. I was in the kitchen putting my food on a plate and then grabbed a beer. When I sat down on the couch, Brian finally stepped inside.

"You gonna close the door or what?"

"I'm waiting on you to invite me in. You act like you don't see my ass. Passing a nigga up with food in your hand and ain't offer me none. I don't know where you at in the head right now. So, I'm staying over here until you let me know."

"Man, get yo' sensitive ass in here."

"Shut up," he said, closing the door. He sat down on the other side of the couch and looked around. "So, what you up to today? You need help with any of this?" Brian pointed to the many stacks of boxes.

"Look, don't come up in here like you tryna hang. We both know who sent you. Tell her, I ain't talking to her until we are face to face like we should be."

"What?" he asked, playing dumb.

I glanced at him and saw that stupid ass face he made whenever he lied. We all knew it. If anyone needed to know the truth and Brian had the answers, we'd go to him and find what we needed to know whether he was honest or not. Unfortunately, he couldn't help himself. Fortunately for everyone else, he didn't know that we could read him.

"There's beer in the fridge," I let him know.

"Look, Dee is on my back because she's been talking to Kim all last night and even this morning. Both of them won't stop until I try to talk some sense into you. That's my story. Give me something good to relay to the women and we ain't gotta talk about none of it."

Is this fool losing his shit? When did he become a message boy? And for the women? I started flipping through the channels and randomly stopped on some crabbing show. I turned the volume up a few levels to be very clear that I was ignoring him.

After I finished my food, I got up and made me another plate. Brian's phone kept beeping, which meant that his master was texting him about me.

"Do you need me to call your wife? She doesn't have to keep texting you while you're still here. Or is it a group text with my soon-to-be ex? I know how y'all like to talk."

"It's not even like that. Dee wants me to stop by the store before going home," he explained before his phone beeped again.

"Okay, that one was about you. She said Kim is worried and wants me to call her, so she can talk to you."

I put my hand out for his phone. Brian got up and went into the kitchen. I called Denise and told her that Kim was blocked on my phone until she brought her ass home. It wasn't true, but it would give them something to gossip about. After going back and forth a little, she let me off the hook.

Denise was a good woman, but she needed to back off. All of this was between me and my lady. She and Brian shouldn't be in the middle. Then again, everybody was drinking the Kool-Aid that Kim made on a regular. They ate up all the bullshit innocent act she'd put on to make me look like the asshole. I could admit that it was occasionally the truth, but definitely not this time.

Brian took his phone back when he sat down with his food.

"Man, I don't even know why you and Denise are getting involved with our business," I told him.

"It's not like I want to be. Being that those two are so close, when one is going through something, they both go through it. Now my wife is all caught up in your drama and I gotta hear her mouth. She asked me to come over and talk to you. I really want to chill and stay out of it. You and Kim are grown ass people capable of figuring this shit out on your own."

"Well, I'm glad we are on the same page. No one needs to check on me or lecture me about how wrong and selfish I'm being. Kim got it covered with backup from my mom. I've heard it enough. My brother needs to stay my brother and not try to get on me about it too."

"I get it. With all the women on you, someone needs to have your back."

"Exactly," I said, finishing off my beer.

"But, bro. Having your back would imply that I agree with your approach about this whole thing and I don't."

He caught me right after stuffing my mouth. "What?" I barely got out through the food.

"From what I heard, you were crazy disrespectful and pissed about her going to work."

"Hold on. That's not—"

"Kim is like family and it's a little disheartening when she calls my wife in tears over some shit you said or did. I don't like getting between you two, but I don't understand your frustration over something so temporary."

"Nigga, it's two months and we literally moved in together two days ago. How would it not be frustrating? I asked her not to go and she never even considered it. Am I supposed to just deal with it? Kim has no regard for me and that's what pissed me off the most. We didn't discuss it before she made the decision. I was only informed about something that was important enough for us to have to agree upon. You don't think she did anything wrong?"

"I didn't say that. It's the way it was relayed to me. They acted like you were calling her all kinds of names and cussing her out over it."

"Yeah, I did. I was pissed."

"About her taking her job seriously? Maybe she didn't have a choice," he suggested.

"She had a fucking choice and she made the wrong one."

Brian faced me. "What does that mean?"

"Nothing man. You are one of them. I can't even talk to you anymore."

"Bullshit. You can't talk to me because you know you're wrong," he argued and sat up straight again.

"How?"

"Overreacting as usual. You call me sensitive, but you are always in your feelings about everything and then you blow the fuck up and no one can say anything to you."

"Man, whatever."

"See," he said.

I took my plate and bottle to the kitchen to throw it away. Two more seconds and Brian's ass would be kicked out. How the hell did we end up arguing about this shit? Kim managed to screw up so much by making choices that didn't only involve her.

Brian came into the kitchen to put his stuff in the trash, then stood there as if he wanted me to say something.

"You and your woman need to leave," I told him, grabbing another beer.

"What?"

"Some kind of way she is here speaking through you and I don't appreciate being double-teamed."

His restrained laugh was most likely fighting with my reasoning. I almost laughed my damn self, but I was serious.

"Ay, I'm only trying to get your side of things," he said.

"It sounds like you already made up your mind that I am in the wrong. I told you what I needed to say."

"Let me ask you this. Why are you so pissed about a two-month wait when you will be getting married soon anyway? You will have the rest of your lives together."

"That's not the point. Kim has no respect for me in this relationship. How am I supposed to take that?"

"If you really thought that, then why the hell would you ask her to marry you? You know damn well you won't find anyone better. Go apologize to her and make this right so they can get off me about it. Visit her. It's only Colorado. The way you're acting, you'd think she'd be on the other side of the planet for years."

We went back into the living room with beers in our hands. It was quiet for a minute. I felt defeated and a little bad for how she had to leave. The whole morning of her flight played in my head and it pissed me off again.

"So, if Denise had to go out of town for work for a month and—"

"Ahh, come on man," he said.

"Nah, listen. If she had to leave and knew about it but didn't talk to you first, how would you feel? For real."

Brian didn't say anything.

"Or better yet, if she had a choice to stay, but chose to go before ever mentioning it to you, that wouldn't piss you off?" I asked again.

"Yeah, I'd be mad at how it was done but if I couldn't do anything about it, what's the point? I would make sure she doesn't do it again and everything would be all good."

"That's what you say now, but when it's happening, it's not that easy to blow off."

"I hear you."

He left about an hour later. I told him I'd call Kim before the night was over so Denise would calm down.

I didn't understand these women. They always had each other's back even when they were wrong. Then again, I couldn't remember them ever claiming to be wrong about anything. Maybe that was the real problem.

ᑭᑭᑭ

I VISITED MY MOM AFTER WORK. SHE GAVE ME NO choice by threatening to throw away a peach cobbler she made for me yesterday. Mom—another woman— was mad at me. My broken promise to stop by the previous weekend was the cause. I recognized the attempted ambush and backed out at the last minute.

My sisters were home from school over the weekend and being bombarded with the "why did you" or "you should've" crap was not inviting. The peach cobbler was also trap, but at least I would only have to face one woman today.

My mom took a container out of the fridge. "How's the new place? When will I be able to see it?" she asked.

"It's cool. You can come by anytime. You know that."

"Y'all not going to have a housewarming or anything?" she asked while preparing me some cobbler.

"Ma, I can't have a party without my roommate."

She glared at me. I sat straight up so it wouldn't seem like I was being a smart ass.

"Roommate, huh? You two are still at it?"

"Not really."

"My ass. No one calls their fiancée a roommate."

"Why you gotta cuss at me? I'm only stating facts."

Mom tilted her head to the side. It made me nervous. I'm a grown ass man. What can she do to me for speaking my truth?

The microwave beeped, and she sat down at the table without going to it. She looked at me that way she did before she'd hand me my ass on a platter and I suddenly regretted giving in to the cobbler lure.

I walked to the microwave and got the plate. "Do you have any ice cream?"

She scoffed before sucking her teeth. I opened the freezer and found some. I put a spoon of it on top of the cobbler and sat down across from her.

When I put the first spoon in my mouth, she rolled her eyes.

"So, Kim got you mad still?" I asked.

"No, son. You got me mad. I raised you better than this."

"Better than what? I'm pissed off. Is that not allowed?"

"I heard all the things you said to her and I didn't like any of it."

What the hell was she talking about? Everybody acted like they were in the damn room when Kim left. We had an argument. So what?

"She recorded you cussing her out and sent it to me," she said. I dropped my spoon. "Yeah, Trenton. I heard every name and foul word you said to that girl. And for what? She loves you and she stayed with you after all that you put her through over the years. How could you be like that? What if she leaves you over this? I know I would."

My chest started hurting. I felt like I couldn't breathe.

That bitch recorded us? Why the fuck would she do that shit? And sent it my mom of all people.

"I need to get home, Ma. I will see you later," I said, getting up from the table.

"You didn't finish your food."

"I can't eat anymore."

She got up and followed me to the door. "Don't do anything stupid, Trenton. Kim is a smart girl. You keep messing up with her, she will be gone."

"If that's what has to happen, it's fine with me. I'll see you."

I gave her a kiss and left. I almost felt bad about how I acted. However, this had to be the lowest shit Kim had ever pulled. Getting my mom involved was bad enough but recording me and shit was on another level.

I was done with the games. Trent the monster, huh? She was painting a picture to everyone and I couldn't defend myself.

My friends and family were on her side. Now I understood why. Anybody can look bad in the middle of a fight. I never thought she'd do me like that. If she wanted a call from me that bad, she'd get one.

When I made it home, I got out my laptop and called her on Skype. She answered with a smile on her face. Seconds later it was gone.

"Hey, babe!"

"Kim." I couldn't even fake like this was a pleasant call. My heart was damn near pumping through my shirt.

"Okay. If you are calling to argue, I can't. Not tonight. I have a long day tomorrow. We can talk another time."

"Oh, I was giving you time to record the fucking conversation. That's what you do now, right?"

She looked down with that dumb expression. She should've known I'd find out. "Nothing to say?" I asked.

"Trent, I—"

"You want me to look like the villain. You want everyone to be on my back about yelling at you, so they wouldn't pay attention to how fucked up it was for you to up and leave like you did. Isn't that right? Kim never does a damn thing wrong. Even if she does, Trent is the one who overreacts. No matter what I do, I'm the bad guy. And you pile it on for everyone, don't you?"

"No, it's—"

"My mom, though? You sent a recording of us fighting to my mom? And I'm supposed to be okay with that? You can do or say anything no matter how I feel about it. As soon as I disagree or get a little loud, I'm the problem."

"Trent, just—"

"No! I hope you have a good life up there. I hope you have to stay there forever. I will put your shit in storage and send you the bill. I don't need this shit from you. Just know that you fucked all of this up. Being sneaky and shit is low. And for anyone who is listening, Kim is the one who has the problems. It's not me. I'm done with the games."

I slammed my laptop shut. Minutes later, my phone was blowing up. Yeah, right. I left to get something to eat. Afterward, I got in the shower and took my ass to bed. Fuck whoever will come at me tomorrow about this shit.

CHAPTER FOUR

Kim

TODAY WAS MY FIRST DAY. THE OFFICE BUILDING was beautiful. It was on the twelfth floor and all you saw were the gorgeous mountains nearby.

I had a meeting with the heads of the other departments. We discussed the plan that Mrs. Roland already shared with me. Lunch was provided too.

There were a lot of greetings and handshaking going around, but it went very well. My first interviews were scheduled for tomorrow morning. It would be the candidates' second interview. Mrs. Roland and I handled many of the first ones over the phone before I came here.

Interviews were not really my thing. I've been in the room whenever they were held, but not to do most of the talking. Ms. Linda and Mrs. Roland had that part down. I had to only do the research on candidates' education, work history, backgrounds, and handle the paperwork with those transitioning in or out of the company.

My apartment was a freaking condo. I wished I could show it off to somebody, anybody. It was that nice. I assumed I'd be in an extended stay hotel or something.

Mrs. Roland made sure I was taken care of. We talked about Trent not feeling this separation and I guess she felt bad about it. There was a lot of work to get done, but I couldn't help but wonder what I would be going back home to in a couple of months.

Trent had me all messed up. I arrived in Denver three days ago and had been calling him plenty each day. He wouldn't answer my calls or texts. I even had Brian talk to him but still no luck.

What the hell was I trying so hard for? That bastard didn't come home the night before I left. Then an hour before I needed to be at the airport, he came into the house with break-fast only for himself and gave me the damn silent treatment.

I assumed that he would be dropping me off at the airport to see me off, but nope. Trent could be an asshole, but that was too much. While he ignored me, I explained how I didn't want to leave my car at the airport and pay parking fees for such a long time.

Every point that needed to be made was made on how he should drop me off. The fact that we wouldn't see each other for a while was the last excuse. I could fly home on the week-ends or he could come to see me, but I had the feeling that neither of us would be willing to do that anyway. So, I called a cab.

To get his attention, I started opening his boxes and throwing shit around the house. I put my phone on record, so he'd know how he did me and would have no questions if I got my stuff and moved out as soon as I returned.

One of his boxes had a basketball in it, so I threw it toward him in the kitchen while he was eating. It bounced at the perfect angle because when it left the ground, it hit him in the face. He went completely off. That man called me all kinds of names; bitch included. I was almost scared, but I didn't let him know it.

He told me how he felt as if I didn't already know, but this time the disrespect surpassed my boundaries. I took my things to the door and waited for my ride.

No goodbye kiss or even a hug. Not that I expected it. That motherfucker went into the master bedroom when he was done with his rant and locked the door. To see him act like this over something so trivial and short-term had me all the way in my feelings.

Luckily, I saw my parents the night before. My mom behaved better than at the so-called dinner they gave me. Otherwise, I would've left Houston on bad terms with everyone I loved.

Maybe this behavior was why she didn't like Trent. Besides the fact that I used to tell her everything that happened between us. I made a mistake in doing that because she developed a hatred for him that I couldn't reverse.

After my flight landed, I called him to see if he'd calmed down, but he still ignored me. Out of anger, I sent the recording of him cussing me out to Sheryl. I messaged her that if I never saw her again, it was because of her son and that it would take a lot for me to get past his behavior.

I told her about the basketball because it really was an accident. I wasn't trying to hit him. It was funny as hell, but still an accident. We talked about it and she was appalled at Trent as well. His rage was getting out of control.

Even after all of that, I kept trying to reach out to him. Like a dumbass, I felt bad about how we left things at the house. When he Skyped me, I thought that there was hope until he spoke.

I didn't care anymore and planned on sending him the engagement ring in the mail. Maybe my dad and brother could get my things from the house before I told him it was over. No need for my stuff to be damaged over any of this. Knowing him, it may have already happened.

My phone rang right on time. I told Denise when I'd be home earlier. "Hey, girl," I said.

"Oh, my gosh. I miss you so much."

"It's only been a few days."

"Yeah, but now I can't invite you over when Brian goes out. I'm so lonely."

"How are you lonely, crazy?"

"Um, your man keeps making my man go out with him every freaking night. You know Brian. He acts like he can't let anyone down."

"What?"

"Yes, girl."

"Sorry, Dee. I had no idea. That idiot still hasn't answered any of my calls. He's still mad at me for leaving."

"According to Brian, Trent is mad at you for throwing a ball in his face."

I burst out laughing. It wasn't planned, but the visual was so worth it. Man, I wish it would've busted his lip or something. Maybe his idiot behavior would be justified a little bit.

"You wrong for that," she said, giggling.

"He deserved worse."

"He's also still pissed about you going to his mom."

"I ain't got time for him to be mad about other people seeing him for who he is."

"Hell, I didn't know he could get that mad at you. No wonder his mama couldn't keep it to herself when she heard it. That was a totally different man on that recording."

"I've been trying to tell y'all. He always talking about I play the victim like he doesn't do anything wrong. He gets mad at me and accuses me of doing the exact thing that he does. I don't have to play the victim after everyone hears both sides."

"You need to come back home so the two of you can get it together."

"The hell. I tried enough. After all that I have forgiven, it has come down to this. We cannot get married anymore. I don't even want to go back to him."

"Kim, don't say that. You don't mean it."

"Yes, the hell I do. You know what we've been through."

"That was years ago. You moved on together."

"Didn't you say he and Brian had been out back- to-back nights?"

"Yeah, so?"

"So, the last time he cheated, where was he always going?" I asked.

It was quiet for a few moments. "You don't think he'd do that to you again, do you?"

"I don't doubt it for a second. He won't answer my calls and he is going out to clubs and whatnot. The last time, it was over something smaller than what we have been going through lately. If he felt justified in fucking around back then, there's no way he isn't doing it again."

"But Brian is with him. He wouldn't let him do that without saying anything."

"I love Brian and all, but men are still men. They are too close for him to betray his trust if something did go down. Like you said, he doesn't like disappointing people. Ratting on Trent's cheating ass would probably ruin their friendship."

"Uh-unh, my baby wouldn't allow it to go that far. You are family to us. There is no way. If Trent was doing you bad, I'd at least know about it by now."

"So, Brian goes home with Trent, too?"

"No. He comes home to me."

"Exactly! How would he know if Trent didn't invite some hoe after they left? He can't be there for everything. I know Trent enough to see it for what it is. We are done."

Denise thought the best of everyone. I tried to make or damn near force my relationship with Trent to work all these years. Now, it seemed like we'd outgrown each other. What fools were we to try to slap a marriage on top of this mess?

After talking to Denise for another hour, my mind was made up on ending things. Whenever I returned to Houston, I'd get another place. The house was in Trent's name. I was supposed to be adding myself to the lease later. Oh, well.

I texted my dad and brother to see if they would be okay getting my stuff. Everything was in boxes. My furniture was in a storage room I rented before the move. We agreed to use Trent's furniture right now and mine when we bought a house. He claimed his furniture was more neutral because mine wasn't some boring color.

My dad called minutes after I sent the text. He wanted to check on me. I understood it was an odd request especially after fighting against them so hard to accept my personal decisions.

Without going into details, I told him that they were right. I needed them to move my things so that we wouldn't shack up and would wait until marriage. Lying didn't feel great, but my mom would get too much satisfaction in finding out that Trent and I were over.

ᛕᛕᛕ

THE WEEK HAD GONE BY WITH MANY NEW HIRES. One of them was "make you want to drop your panties" fine. The way I was feeling about that fool back home, I may have smiled too hard during the interview. He was dreamy, like straight from the big screen dreamy. There wasn't a wedding ring on his finger either.

The guy was a great match for the position he was applying for and got the job. I didn't look forward to seeing him every day. Hopefully, we wouldn't bump into each other often because I was prone to having sexual dreams about men that looked like him. Especially when I hated Trent.

Mrs. Roland and I did a morning meeting twice a week either over the phone or live video. She wanted to keep an eye on me and to actually see me when we briefly talked about anything personal. I kept it short when it came to that part of our talks. It wasn't important because I was there to do my job and no man was going to stop me or make me feel bad for it.

I presented the lineup of candidates to interview next week. One of them was for my job. Once they were trained and had a decent size staff for the HR department, I would head back home.

With the peace I'd experienced since I got here, it wasn't an exciting idea. Trent and I hadn't spoken or texted each other since he hung up on Skype. Until he had something to say to me, things would stay this way. Every time we had an argument, I'd be the one to break the ice even when I didn't cause the problem. Not this time.

Trent

My lady hadn't called me in over a week. I messed up bad. Mom sent me the recording she'd gotten from Kim. I heard myself and it fucked with my head.

In the moment, it didn't seem as bad as that recording made it sound. I wasn't denying that it was me yelling and cussing at her, but damn.

I wholeheartedly believed my actions were justified in the situation until I heard the way I talked to her that day. If some random nigga came at her like that, I would've fucked him up.

Kim should've called me back by now. She always came to me and then we'd make up. I didn't know where her head was. If I did call her, would she even answer? Shit, I wouldn't. Tripping the way that I did, I hoped a little time and space would go a long way.

Did she miss me?

Granted, I hung up in her face last week. She probably thought I was still mad. As much as I wanted to be right this time, I blew it. Everyone else knew it before I did. Then my mom let me have it with a long text after I left her house mad again a couple of nights ago. She attached a download titled *The little boy I didn't raise. Who are you?*

The recording started with me calling my wife-to- be a selfish bitch. I went on yelling that she didn't care about me and that she was basically pushing me to find someone else. It was embarrassing.

I told her to never come back and that I hoped she finds some white guy to get with because she wasn't the type of woman a brother wanted. I said that she wasn't loyal and that she didn't listen like a good woman supposed to.

I didn't know who else heard this message, but it made my ass paranoid. Whenever I saw anyone we both knew, I felt nervous and naked. I would normally stand by my words and actions with no remorse, but this time I went too far.

Last weekend, I convinced Brian to come over every night and chill. Knowing how Kim thought, I wanted her to assume the worst. I asked Brian to lie and tell Denise we were out and about so that Kim would get jealous. That's what I felt she deserved at the time.

He must have told the truth that we had been hanging at my place playing video games and watching old stand-up comedy shows. We'd usually watch something like that if no good games or fights were on.

If Kim fell for it, she would've called a million times. Since she didn't, Brian must not have gone with my plan. He was so damn soft when it came to his woman. He couldn't lie or keep a secret to save his life.

This weekend, I wanted to go somewhere. So, last night we went to some new bar with the biggest TV screens on this side of town. It was pretty hype with almost a club environment. With plenty of temptation present, we had rolled out sooner than I'd planned.

The women were so forward sending us shots. Maybe I'd been taken for so long that I was unaware of this shift. Men used to go after women, not being the ones pursued. I didn't know how it made me feel. One of us probably would've been drugged or some shit if we had stayed longer.

After I dropped Brian off, I went home. With the recording fresh in my mind, I poured me a glass of vodka on ice and watched TV. Nothing blocked my vicious tone replaying in my head.

I needed to lay off the liquor since I had to work the next day. But whenever I reached the bottom of my glass, I refilled it. I couldn't remember what was on the TV when I fell asleep. I was out.

ᗕᗕᗕ

THE MORNING CAME QUICK. BARELY ABLE TO GET UP, I called in for work and went back to sleep. A few hours later I heard someone opening my door. I jumped up ready to fight, then Brian walked into my living room.

"Ooh, damn. You're home? I thought you were at work," Brian said.

"How the hell did you get in here? What are you doing?" I asked. Another man entered. "Oh, hey, Mr. Duncan," I greeted him.

"Trent," he responded, sternly.

Mr. Duncan looked like he wanted to beat my ass. Kim's brother was behind them but didn't speak. They must have known what went down. What the hell were they doing in my house?

"Um, so..." Brian barely said.

"My daughter wants us to get her things out of here and that's what we came to do," Mr. Duncan told me.

"Really, Brian?" I asked.

Confused wasn't even the half of it. Why was he with

them? And when did this nigga get a key? My head began spinning, so I sat back down. What the fuck?

"Can y'all wait outside for a few minutes? Let me talk to him first," Brian said to the other men.

I saw them leave from the corner of my eye. The door was open the whole time and the sun forced me to look away. When they left, Brian walked over to the couch and sat down, looking like a kid about to confess to a parent after he got caught.

"Brian, what the fuck are y'all doing here, man?"

"Ay, this is all Kim. I had no idea until this morning. Denise got the key to your place from Kim. She asked me to meet Kim's people over here so they could move her stuff out. I didn't know how to tell you, so I didn't. I figured you'd find out when you got home from work."

"Nigga, why you always doing this shit to me?"

"Doing what?"

"Do you have any ounce of nuts left? Or did Denise take everything?"

I really wanted to know. This motherfucker always did what he was told. He acted like he couldn't say something if he didn't agree. Those women had his punk ass wrapped around their fingers.

"Man, whatever," he said, swiping his hand at me.

"Nah, I'm serious. You never have my back with this kind of shit. You just obey your master with no questions."

He stood up and I did the same. "You got shit all twisted. When you fuck up, I gotta help fix it because of Denise. This time, I won't. Kim wants her things and I don't fucking blame her. So, yes I am helping her out because she deserves better and finally realized it."

"What the fuck did you say?"

"Oh, now you can't hear?"

I pushed him, and he took a few unbalanced steps backwards. He pushed me hard. I tripped on the corner of the couch and knocked over the end table.

"Muthafucka!" I yelled.

"Yeah, we'll see who has nuts if you keep coming at me crazy," he threatened me.

Brian was in a fighting stance that I wasn't ready for. Something happened when I fell. My stomach got shook or some shit because I dashed for the guest bathroom and barely made it to the toilet to throw up.

Everything went quiet except when I gagged with more of my guts flowing out. I hated this shit. Brian didn't come to check on me. He must've been too heated. That nigga was always asking, "Are you okay?" or "Do you need help?" It seemed weak to me, but when he didn't do it this time, it felt cold.

I flushed the toilet and sat against the wall. I could hear the three of them talking, but not clearly. Footsteps were all around the place and doors were creaking open. Kim told me to put some type of oil on the hinges when we first moved in. Of course, I didn't listen.

All her boxes were labeled with her name and the contents. I didn't understand why she put her name on them, but now I see. She must've known this would happen. Maybe this was part of the plan all along if I didn't act the way she wanted me to. I should've unpacked her stuff, so they wouldn't know what to take.

The front of my head felt like a sledgehammer hit it all of a sudden. I leaned my head against the wall and closed my eyes. I wanted to get up and fight back and tell them to get the hell out. I wanted to stop them from taking anything. When my body gave up, so did I.

For a while I sat there on the floor. I dozed off a few times. The last time, someone knocked on the bathroom door.

"Are you still breathing?" It was Mr. Duncan.

"Does it matter?" I asked.

"I'll take that as a yes," he said, before walking away.

A few minutes later, the front door slammed. They were gone.

I picked myself up and slowly walked to my bed. They took everything she had. None of her things were unpacked since she left days after we moved in. It was back to a bachelor's pad.

As hard as I tried to fight it, a few tears came down my face. It was anger, then it had hit me that this meant Kim was gone. She left me, left me. I had fucked up for real.

My body still felt weak. I didn't know where my phone was so that I could call her. When I tried to get up to look for it, I couldn't. I needed to sleep this shit off. I could figure out what to do later with a clear head.

It was almost seven o'clock when I woke up. I showered and came out starving. I found my phone dead in the kitchen. Once I got it on the charger, I ordered Jimmy John's. I drank from the gallon jug of water.

The phone had to have been off all day and still had no missed calls or texts from anyone. Were they all in on a joke that I hadn't caught on to? No one checked on me. Not Kim. Not Brian. For good reason. I almost fought my brother. And for what?

My mom surprised me the most. She was notorious for calling and texting too much. There was nothing from her.

The food came, and I sat in front of the TV stuffing my face, contemplating whether to call Kim. She was at the top of the list of people I needed to make up with. She seriously got her family to come here and remove her from my life. Kim knew better than that. I wasn't going to let it happen like this.

We'd been through too much shit for this to be the end of it all. I loved her, and I wanted her to be my wife. No matter what I'd said before now, it had never been so clear to me. I knew I wasn't the best dude on the planet, but she was the best woman.

After everything, she loved me more than I deserved, and I'd be crazy to let her go that easily. Whatever I had to do, it would have to be big. Much bigger than the mess I made that got us here in the first place. No matter what, I was going to get my lady back.

CHAPTER SIX

I'D BEEN IN DENVER FOR THREE WEEKS. IT HAD BEEN super busy at the office. By the time I got home, I was dog tired.

A few of us girls went out for dinner a couple times this week. I was invited again tonight but couldn't do it. My body wasn't old or anything, but it was telling me to finally get a full night's sleep.

All this shit with Trent had me up most nights. I didn't talk to him, but the stress made me restless. Those damn movie channels were part of the problem, too. After you finish one good movie, another one came on. The cycle wouldn't end. Next thing I knew, I was only getting four hours of sleep.

This weekend was my trip back home. I missed my family more than anything. When they were minutes away, I would pass on seeing them until another time. Now I couldn't see them at all.

My mom didn't make it any better. She'd been in the best mood after I admitted breaking up with Trent. She was a piece of work. Now that her daughter was back in her good graces and not shacking up, she wanted to be best friends. We must've video chatted almost every other day with her calling in between.

Even Sheryl called to check on me. Of course, she wanted to talk about her son and that was when I'd cut the call short.

Friday came, and I was off to Houston. My dad picked me up from the airport and took me straight to Buffalo Wild Wings. We made plans to eat out so that we'd make it home extra late and I could avoid my mom for at least one night at their house.

Dad knew how much she could get on my nerves and he also never turned down hot wings and beer. He told me about the day they got my stuff from Trent's place. It was his new favorite story to tell because he claimed he was ready to fight Trent if he got out of line. We ate and talked about work. I enjoyed this responsibility and hoped to do more of it when I got back home for good.

We went to the house and sure enough, Mom had fallen asleep on the couch. Mission accomplished.

The next morning, I woke up to the heavenly smell of someone cooking for me without me getting dressed and leaving the house for it. I missed this part the most after moving out. The independence felt even better, but having your mom cook breakfast before you get up was the best.

During breakfast, she asked me what I'd be doing for the day because she wanted to spend time with me. Denise had plans for us later, so I was free. Apparently, she'd already planned my morning before she had asked that question.

After an hour, we were ready to hit the town with some pampering. She took us to get a couples massage, manicures and pedicures, shopping, lunch, and a movie. When we got home, I was ready for a nap.

I'd forgotten how much fun it was to hang out with my mom. We were so busy butting heads because of my relationship with Trent that we lost this part of our own relationship.

It was an amazing day that I almost wished didn't have to end.

My sister stopped by and we chilled a little until she had to run some errands. We played my favorite card game, speed. She could never beat me when we were younger and that hadn't changed today. We must've played six times before she gave up.

After Keisha left, I got ready to head over to Denise's. I warned her not to try anything stupid because she was still on that "you two need to work it out" crap.

When I got there, I saw some cars outside their house. None of them were Trent's so it was cool. I called her to let her know I was outside. She came out to my car asking why I didn't come to the door. I needed her to explain what I was walking into.

It was a couples game night that she was hosting. Denise claimed it was scheduled before I told her I'd be coming to town. She and some ladies from church planned to do this to have fun without having to be out of their comfort zone.

These couples were drinking Christians. Not alcoholics, but the sipping kind. They were too afraid someone would see them from the church and judge them. It was silly, but that's how they felt. So, the start of Couples Game Night began. This was their second time meeting up and they only did it once a month. I remembered skipping out on that invitation last time.

"Get out of the car and come inside," she told me.

"It sounds nice and all, but it might be too awkward for me," I admitted.

"It's not like you don't know these people."

"Exactly my point. I will get the questions or sympathy stares when they find out I'm single again."

"Ain't nobody worried about you. Come on. I wanted to spend some time with you this weekend and this is it, so get your butt out the car," she said, opening my door.

"Ugh, fine."

Every fear or insecurity I had was for nothing. She was right, no one cared. They acted happy to see me and only asked about work and Denver. It was like Denise prepped them not to ask about Trent because absolutely no one did.

There were three other couples besides Brian and Denise. Everyone had a drink in their hand, but it was light sipping. She only had wine cooler type drinks, beer, and sweet wine. Nothing with a very high alcohol content.

The food was the bomb. My girl made my favorites, shrimp scampi with cheddar biscuits. After I ate a plate of real food, I snacked on the fruit, cheese, and crackers tray. 90's R&B played in the background. It went great and I had a blast.

After everyone left, I got ready to head out. I went to the restroom first and when I came out, Trent was standing in their living room.

"Nope. Not doing it," I said walking past him to the front door.

He caught up with me and grabbed my arm.

"Babe, please."

"I'm not your babe. I'm a selfish bitch, remember."

I heard someone whisper, "Damn."

"Denise, I can't believe you had him come here. I told you how I felt, and I meant it. Everybody can't stay together, okay," I declared, getting loud.

"I didn't," she told me.

"My bad, Kim. He asked what we were doing, and I mentioned you were here with us," Brian confessed. "Thanks a lot," I said, rolling my eyes.

"Can I talk to you for a minute?" Trent asked me. "For what, you said all you needed to say weeks ago and nothing since then. I'm done."

"In my defense, you wouldn't answer my calls," he claimed.

"Yeah, because they were two weeks too late."

"Um, we're going to go in the back, so you guys can have some privacy," Denise told us.

"No need. I'm leaving. I will see you guys next time."

I hugged Denise and Brian and walked right past Trent. He tried to touch me. I moved from his reach and left. I got to my car before he came out of the house. He ran up on me and grabbed me from behind.

"Get the fuck off me, Trent," I yelled.

"Okay, okay. I'm sorry," he said, backing up with his hands slightly in the air.

I opened the car door and got in. He stood in the way of me and the door, so I couldn't close it. I lay my head back on the headrest. I didn't have the energy to try and move him out of the way.

"Kim, I know I am the last person you want to see or talk to, but I want you to know how sorry I am for everything. I was an asshole to the nth power and I don't even know how to make it right. All I know is that I don't want to lose you."

I rolled my eyes and sucked my teeth. He had plenty of time to do this before now. It's not my fault he chose to stay in asshole mode. Oh, well.

Trent got on both of his knees and grabbed my hand. I pulled it back. He raised an eyebrow.

"You're not wearing your ring."

"Why would I? If you want it, I'll mail it to you when I go back. I don't need it."

"I don't want it. I gave it to you because I want to spend the rest of my life with you."

"I'm pretty sure I don't want to spend mine with you. I'd rather not be disrespected every time you throw a fucking temper tantrum."

"Kim, I understand where you're at, but please let me make it up to you. This will never happen again. I promise."

"I don't believe you. So..."

"Alright, Kim. I guess I have to accept that."

"Yep. Now, can you move so I can go?"

Trent moved without saying another word and finally let me drive off. I played loud music to distract myself from thinking about that idiot on the way to my parents' house.

My dad was still up when I got in. We talked about what happened and all he told me was that I had to make my own decisions and he'd support me either way. In other words, he was of no help.

The next day we went to church and then out for lunch. Later mom made Sunday dinner and had the family over. I got to see my grandmother who just over a month ago damned me to hell for planning to move in with Trent. The evening went by so fast that I almost missed my alarm to leave for the airport. I said my goodbyes and headed out.

ᗃᗃᗃ

WORK WAS A GREAT DISTRACTION FROM everything, but every day when I got home, a gift had been delivered to my apartment. Trent sent flowers, candy, a bracelet, and a card with each one apologizing for his behavior. The bracelet was a nice touch, however, I needed to stand my ground for him to really get it. His gifts would not buy me off.

He texted sweet messages all day. I couldn't remember the last time he worked this hard for me to accept his apology. Even when he cheated, he gave up after a few days and we were broken up for months. For some reason, this felt worse. Cheating was a major deal breaker, but the level of disrespect he reached took the cake.

Every call went unanswered if his name popped up. Brian called me once with Trent on the line, so now he was on my bad side. I didn't need him helping my current enemy.

Denise called herself trying to be a mediator. These were the times that I hated their perfect asses. Just because they loved each other's dirty drawers didn't mean that Trent and I had the same relationship.

Brian and Trent were two different species and once everyone realized it, they'd see that it was not so easy to go back to how things were. I refused to brush shit under the rug any longer. The pile had gotten so high that I couldn't see past it. We'd have to make some major changes in ourselves to really make this work and I didn't see that happening with him.

Friday came and so did another package. It had a huge bear in it with more candy. This time no note was included.

I ordered Chinese food and a newly released movie on cable. As soon as the food came, Trent called again. I ignored the call and went to the door to get my dinner. When I opened it, Trent was standing there with a vase of flowers.

"Hey, baby!"

"What the hell are you doing at my door?"

I was hungry for my orange chicken and was not in the mood for this. Trent stood there with that dumbass, lost look.

"You won't answer my calls, so I had to come and see you," he explained.

Nobody but Denise gave him my address. She was starting to make me hate her. We were supposed to be tight, but she wouldn't stop interfering.

"The other fifty times I pressed ignore didn't convey the clear message that I don't want to see you?"

We still stood in the doorway. He looked over my head inside the apartment, so I stepped into the hall and kept the door slightly open with my back against it.

"Damn, is it really like that? I know that I pissed you off but aren't you a little too mad for too long."

"Nigga? You don't—"

Someone turned the corner onto my hall. It was the delivery guy. He gave me my food and went on his way.

"Welp, I guess I'll see you some other time. I don't want this to get cold." I went inside and let the door close behind me.

As soon as I placed the food on the kitchen counter, he called and knocked at the same time.

I was both surprised and touched that he came all this way unannounced. Either way, he remained on my shit list. Trent needed to really fear losing me because that's where we were. He acted like it was a game. I opened the door quickly.

"Kim, come on. Could you at least let me come in for a minute to talk?" He handed me the vase.

"Now, why on Earth would I do that?"

The puppy dog eyes and bottom lip poking out was his last resort. He looked so stupid that I laughed a little.

"See, I knew you still loved me."

"Boy, please. You look dumb as hell. I can laugh and still hate you."

"Can I come in, please?"

"Ugh, whatever. You aren't getting any of my food, though."

I walked away and let the door hit him on the way in. He walked into the living room and looked around. I made myself a plate of food and grabbed a wine cooler from the fridge.

On the way to the couch, I told him to start talking because I had plans and he was wasting my time standing there.

After apologizing a hundred times, I let him sit down and watch the movie with me in silence. It was a horror thriller that I regretted renting.

Too many times I wanted to lay in his arms and cover my face. I managed to keep it together through the whole thing.

We usually talked after a movie like that, but this time it was quiet.

"Well, that's over. You should leave now. I have a long day tomorrow," I told him.

"On a Saturday?"

"Yep."

"Oh, okay. Can I come by tomorrow and see you for a bit?"

Trent gave me bedroom eyes as if it would do anything. It was not going down like that tonight. This boy had another thing coming if he thought all it would take was one flight and some gifts for the plum fool behavior he put on before. I told him that I'd see if I had time for him tomorrow and would let him know then. We walked to the door and he left.

Trent

I STOOD OUTSIDE THE DOOR FOR ABOUT THREE minutes before knocking on it again. It wouldn't be right to let her go to bed one more night hating me. Everything I knew how to do, I did, but she wouldn't let up. Yes, I messed up, but I knew I'd done way worse things in the past and she forgave me.

Kim opened the door looking like she wanted to punch me in my face. I wished she would at least do it so I could take some of the hurt off of her. She really hated me. There had to be a way to break down the wall between us.

"Trenton, what is it now?"

"So, I didn't realize you'd still be like this when you saw me. The whole thing played out a lot differently in my head. Which is kind of why I didn't book a hotel room."

"And?"

"I wanted to know if I could stay here with you?"

"Boy, please. There are plenty of hotels you can go to."

"But I caught a cab here. I don't have a car."

"Well, it sounds to me like you have the number to the cab service already. Call them again and get a ride."

Damn, she was quick with it. I had run out of excuses.

"Look, I promise not to bother you at all. If you would let me sleep on the couch or even the floor, I could keep you safe tonight."

"You do realize that I've been here a while without you and felt safer than I do now."

"Please?"

"Why do you even want to? After all this time, don't you want to be done with us?"

"After all what time? It's only been a month."

"That was long enough for me to see that we should stop wasting each other's time."

Being that it was so late, I asked if I could come inside to talk about it. She agreed.

I stood in her living room hoping she'd have more to say about anything at this point, but the TV was the only thing making a sound. Kim walked around the place doing things as if I was invisible.

"Kim?"

"Yes," she answered, making her way to the couch after what sounded like brushing her teeth.

"Please talk to me. Tell me what I did wrong, so I can fix it. Things can't end like this, babe."

"They can and should. I have waited for you to grow up for so long. Through the good and the bad, I was always there. I can't even say why anymore. That's probably what changed. I don't know why I take anything from you. Now, I realized I don't have to."

"What?"

"Boy, you have lied, cheated, and disrespected me with both actions and words. Yet, I stayed hoping you'd be different and then we can truly be happy. I don't remember the last time I was genuinely happy with you. Your last tantrum was all I needed to know that you are who you are and how you are. I cannot change you and I don't want to anymore."

Every word felt like the tip of a sharpened butcher knife pushing deeper and deeper into me.

"Why now? I didn't know you felt like this. I thought we were past all the other stuff. You said so yourself."

"Yeah, I did. That was part of the problem. I lied to keep the peace. I was tired of fighting over the same things. I figured one day you'd get it, but you never did. Honestly, I don't think I forgave you for even half the shit you put me through. Being here without you revealed that to me. You hurt me so much that it's like a mountain in front of me. It's not worth the climb. We both can do better and be better, but not with each other."

"Don't say that. I only want you. Look, I know it's been a lot, but we can get through this. Don't give up on us so easily."

"Trust me, this decision wasn't easy. Your attitude over the last few weeks is what made it clear. It was hard to accept at first and it still is. But maybe we keep confusing a good relationship with the length of it. The years together were long and hard. That doesn't mean that we have something worth anything in the end. All we do is fight. When was it ever consistently good?"

"You can't be for real. It sounds like you hated me the whole time we were together."

"Trent, that's not what I am saying. All of this feels like there was never any real value in what we had. Nothing worth fighting for besides spending time together. We weren't building anything."

"That's not true. At least not for me."

"How so, Trent? Explain to me what we had that's so great. All we do is argue and it ends with you cussing me out and me coming back to you like I was wrong when I wasn't."

What the fuck? I didn't even know who this person was. "Stop acting like you never did anything wrong," I said, raising my voice. Her innocent act had pissed me off.

"See what I mean."

"Whatever. We wouldn't be here if you didn't take this job behind my back," I yelled.

"Okay, Trent. I'm going to sleep."

I grabbed her arm and pulled her closer to me when she walked by.

"Let go," she demanded.

"Wait a minute. I'm sorry for just now and every time before today. I don't know what's wrong with me. I'm tripping."

"Whatever, let me go."

I did. "Please, let's talk."

"I said what I needed to say, and you went back to typical Trent-mode. Everything is on everyone else, never you."

"But that's not wh—"

"Goodnight," she said sternly and walked down the hall.

After laying down on the couch, the conversation played over in my head. I didn't know what to think of all this. What I did know was this couldn't be the end of us.

ɷɷɷ

THE SUN CAME UP AND IT WAS SHINING IN MY FACE through the window. There were no curtains, only slightly opened blinds. I couldn't block it out. Then I heard Kim in the back for a few minutes before she walked into the kitchen fully dressed.

"You leaving?" I asked, sitting up on the couch. "Yeah, I'm meeting a friend for breakfast."

"What friend?"

"It doesn't concern you," she said, looking at me while pouring a glass of water.

"But I thought we could spend a little time together to see how we can, you know, fix things."

"Well, I didn't ask you to. We made these plans before you decided to pop up at my door."

"Please, Kim. I already feel like I'm running out of time with you. Can you give me today?"

She rolled her eyes, then picked up her phone. It looked like she was texting. Her phone dinged seconds after she finished. It'd better not be another nigga on the other end. We hadn't even officially broken up yet.

"Now, what?" she asked.

I asked her where the restroom was, so I could get myself together. When I came out, we decided to go eat breakfast.

At the restaurant, she seemed normal. A smile finally broke through. We talked about work and how she was ready to be back home with everyone else. She didn't mention me as part of the reason.

I told her about the day her people came to the house to take her things. She thought it was much funnier than I did. Kim talked about us as if "we" were the past and I wasn't ready to give up.

We went for a walk in a park and talked a bit more. I convinced her to let me have another chance. She had conditions that I should've seen coming.

The engagement was off, and we'd live separately when she got back. If I came at her wrong, she'd pull the plug. All I needed was the opportunity to show her that we had something worth fighting for. I hated that she didn't feel the same.

The weekend wasn't what I planned but it did feel good to hear her laugh and see that beautiful smile again. We ate out for every meal and chilled. It was a good sign that she at least still enjoyed being around me.

When it came time for me to leave, I felt it was on good terms. I could live with that. We would work this out soon enough.

I got home with a good report for my mom who was on my back about making things right with Kim. My mom said that even if Kim didn't take me back, I had to make sure we were on better terms than when she first left. I knew I had at least accomplished that much.

I made sure Kim didn't go a day without hearing from me and I could tell she appreciated it. Only a few weeks more until she'd be back here, and I could really show her what I was willing to do for her, for us.

A few friends of mine invited me out to play pool at this new bar down the street from Brian's. I called him to come out, but he wasn't sure if Denise would let him. I met up with the guys to get a break from my empty house. Knowing all the making up I'd have to do, no one would see me out for a while when Kim returned.

Halfway through one game, someone tapped me on the shoulder. It was her. I took a few steps back, bumping into the pool table.

"Hey, stranger," she said.

"Uh." I cleared my throat. "H-Hey."

"It's been too long, Trent.".

"Um—" The back of my head had suddenly itched like hell.

"You going to introduce us and start playing? Or do we need to give you two some privacy?" one of the guys said.

"Oh, uh. This is Toni. Toni, these are a bunch of nobod- ies." Everyone laughed. I tried to look at her while avoiding her eyes.

"Can I talk to you real quick?" she asked.

"Um, yeah."

I told the guys I'd be back and that they could finish the

game without me. We found two barstools at the bar to sit.

"You look good," she said, biting the corner of her bottom lip. Toni knew what that used to do to me.

"Thanks. You too."

"It's crazy seeing you here. I've been thinking about you a lot lately and even tried calling, but your number must've changed."

"Oh, yeah I changed it a couple years ago."

"I see. She made you do it," she said, staring at me like she was looking for trouble.

"Nah, I had to because—"

"Dang, Trent. Why are you sweating? Am I making you nervous?" she asked, wiping her hand across my forehead.

"Nah, it's the lights or something. I mean it is a little warm in here."

Toni looked sexier than the last time I saw her, but I knew better than to say so. I needed to find a way back to the table without looking weak.

"So, what have you been up to?" she asked. "Not much, I..."

Brian walked in and spotted me sitting with her. I saw the look on his face and knew I had to get to him before his imagination took off.

"Toni, it was good seeing you again. I have to go, one of my boys just walked in."

"Oh, okay. Can I get..."

I darted toward Brian, leading us to the rest of the guys. The expression on his face told me everything he was thinking, and I had to make sure he didn't leave here with those same thoughts. Brian was my brother, but he had a hard-on for truth even if it was out of context.

"Look, it's not what you think," I assured him.

"Ohhh. My bad, man. I could've sworn you were over there talking to the woman you cheated on Kim with."

"Whoa!" one of my friends said.

"Damn," the other one let out.

"Wait, everybody chill. It's not like that," I told them.

Shit! Why did she have to be here tonight? And looking like that in those jeans? "Can we leave? I'm sure there's somewhere else we can go nearby."

They agreed, and we found another bar two blocks down. The pool tables were taken so we sat around the bar. Everyone's eyes were on me after the bartender handed us our drinks.

"I didn't do anything wrong, man. Stop looking at me like that," I said to Brian.

Unfortunately, I had to explain to everyone else who Toni was and how important it was to steer clear of her. She was the last person I needed to see. That woman was my weakness. It wasn't just her big ass and pretty face.

Toni was a good girl that I went to high school with. Years later, we saw each other at a store and kept in touch. Things got a little out of hand and we crossed the line. It really destroyed things with Kim. I told her that Toni was a random woman and only a one-time thing. I lied to her back then and never admitted the whole truth.

I told Toni I was with someone and she respected it at first. Once she presented herself to me with no strings attached, I took the bait. Next thing I knew, I was staying out later claiming it was for work. She had something that I didn't get with Kim: passion. Toni really wanted me and not only my dick. We were falling, and I got sloppy.

I tried to forget about her and lately, I have, but two years wasn't that long ago. Every part of me remembers every part of her like we never stopped messing around.

Her timing couldn't be worse. I was fighting for a woman who barely wanted me anymore and now the one I knew would love me better had to show her face. Fuck.

ʬʬʬ

I CALLED KIM AFTER WORK SINCE SHE TEXTED ME earlier that she had something important to talk about. Brian must've said something to Denise about Toni. They all knew who she was because I was caught out with her by those two one night when we were having a late dinner.

Denise came at me like Kim probably would've. It was a crazy evening to say the least. Now I had to face Kim about something that wasn't even going on.

After the call, I was all over the place. Kim was asked to stay in Colorado longer and she asked me about it this time. There was no way in hell I would tell her not to stay.

At this point, she could do anything she wanted, and I'd have to be okay with it. The news wasn't great, but what could I do besides give my blessing.

Brian invited me over to play Madden. I'm sure it was to keep tabs on me. I didn't know how much the women knew because of Saint Brian. At least I'd get a good home-cooked meal out of it. Denise was that kind of woman. Even if only one person was coming over, she'd make something whether dinner or appetizers. Girly could cook.

When I got there, it was only the two of us. "Where's the wife?" I asked.

"At her mom's. I was bored and thought you'd be too."

"Yeah right, nigga. You still think I'm messing with ol' girl."

"No, I don't. I believed you the other night."

"Yeah, whatever. Where the food at? I thought I'd be getting fed while whooping yo' ass on this game."

"Like that will ever happen. I'm still undefeated. I ordered some pizza from this new place down the street."

"A'ight, cool."

We finished a beer before the food came and took a break

from the game to eat. Brian turned on ESPN in the living room. Since Denise wasn't around, we didn't have to sit at the kitchen table like a family. She was weird like that.

"So, how you feel about Kim staying longer? She told you last weekend, right?" he asked.

It took me a minute to get my thoughts straight because I was sure I'd heard him wrong. "Last weekend?" I asked.

"Yeah"

I chuckled. Her lying ass never stopped. "Nah, she didn't say anything about it until earlier today. She acted like she just found out and asked how I felt about it. I assumed it was her way of showing me she cared what I thought this time around."

"Damn, man. I didn't know. She told Denise about it last week."

"Muthafucka."

"Ay, wait. Maybe she forgot or something."

"She ain't forget shit. She's the same old selfish Kim."

"Come on, man."

"Come on nothing. I went there pouring my heart out to that girl and she never said shit about this."

"Maybe she had a good reason. It's not like you two were on good terms."

"Kill that. You always be taking her side."

"It's not sides. I don't want you to blow it out of proportion and then have to pay for it later like you always do. Or worse, go mess with that girl again."

I was done with this conversation. Why would he say some shit like that? I swear he acted like these women.

"On that note, I'm out. Don't worry about warning your best friend. I'll talk to her myself."

If she wanted to play games with me like this, then all bets were off.

Kim

T HE PAST TWO WEEKS HAD BEEN WEIRD WITH Trent. Some days he was sweet and others, cold. Today I found out why when I talked to Brian who always seemed to run his mouth at the worst possible time. I was upset for a second, but it wasn't his fault.

I could've told Trent the truth when he was here. At the time, it didn't seem necessary because I didn't believe any of the bullshit he was spewing for us to stay together. He only called me twice after the first few days last week claiming to have been tired after work or forgetting to call. He didn't explain why so many of my calls or texts went unanswered.

Work was wrapping up. The young lady I trained was very sharp and didn't really need me over her shoulder for much longer. The rest of the group for this department were amazing. I almost didn't want to leave them. They were around my age or younger while my office back home was filled with older folks.

Mom prepared a room for me at their house. My stay would be as short as possible. I was determined to find an apartment quickly. My old one didn't have any units available.

Denise called me as soon as I left work. "I'm sending you a picture. Tell me what you think," she said.

I got into my car and checked my messages. It was a picture of Trent at a restaurant with some woman. I froze at the thought of him playing me this whole time with his "let's stay together" act.

"Hello? Kim? Did you get it? Hello?"

I hung up the phone and stared at the image. The angle was a bad one because I couldn't see the woman's face. It wasn't his mom or sisters because of the short hair. The women in his family had big, curly hair.

The drive home was rough. It could be anyone for any reason besides the one my brain kept trying to assume. After all we went through, that definitely couldn't be true. However, the missed calls and behavior the past week made me go back to when he had his last one-night stand. But that would be impossible now, right? He wouldn't be that stupid.

I called him twice and he didn't answer. Denise called me three times before I picked it up. I had to wait until I was home and comfortable before having this talk with her. If I knew anything, she was thinking the same thing I was trying not to.

"What happened?" she asked.

"Girl, I dropped the damn phone in the car and couldn't get it when I was driving," I lied. "Oh, but did you see the picture?"

"Yeah, I don't know who that is," I stated quickly, hoping she'd drop it.

"It's not that girl from last time?"

"I don't think so. I'm not sure, but he wouldn't be having lunch with her."

"Well, Brian said he saw the two of them talking at a bar a couple weeks ago, but Trent told him she only happened to be in the same place at the same time."

"What?"

"Yeah, girl. Then he got mad about you not telling him about staying in Denver longer when he was there with you. I put two and two together and assumed that was probably her."

"Okay, Denise. This is too much. I didn't know he was talking to that bitch again. I need to go."

"Are you okay?"

"No, I'm not. If all that you said is true. I'm really not."

"Sorry, Kim. I hope it's not her at the table with him."

"Yeah, me too. I'll call you back."

What the fuck was going on? That nigga acted like losing me would ruin him. He didn't care about me as much as he led on. If he was seeing someone else, I would never forgive him.

Maybe lying about when I was asked to stay longer was the wrong move, but I made that decision before he decided to show up at my place. It didn't seem like the right thing to bring up while he was begging for us to get back together. Being considered in that type of decision was important to him and I wanted to let him know that I heard him the first time.

I called him once more before bed and he still didn't answer. Either he was too mad to talk, or he was with her. I needed to know, so I sent him the picture Denise took, captioned "Who the fuck is this?"

Minutes later, Trent finally called me. I didn't answer the first time to see if he'd call twice. He did.

"Hello."

"Kim, what the hell is this?" he asked like he didn't already know.

"You tell me. I've been trying to call you forever and then someone sends me a picture of you and this woman. What am I supposed to think?"

"You can think whatever you want. You lied first."

"Hold up. What you mean first?"

"Why you didn't tell me you were already staying?"

"Trent, we were not talking at the time, so it wasn't necessary to tell you. I figured you wouldn't care since you were ignoring me prior to that."

"Excuses, excuses."

"Don't talk to me like that."

"Like what? Like the liar you are. You tried to play me, Kim. You know it."

"I wasn't trying to do anything but protect your feelings. I see it didn't take much for your ass to go back to your old ways. I can't believe you, Trent."

"I didn't do anything."

"Why were you with her? I know that was her."

"Babe, it wasn't what it looked like. I promise."

"So, now I'm babe again?"

"Don't be like that. Yes, I was fucking heated when I found out you took the extension without telling me. My mom calmed me down. Apparently, she knows you better than I do. Even though she told me why you did what you did, I still didn't understand why you felt you couldn't tell me. We were supposed to be starting over and it was like a slap in the face."

"Trent, I'm sorry. You know that wasn't what I was trying to do."

"Yeah, I know."

It was quiet for a few moments. The elephant hadn't been discussed enough, but he seemed to have calmed down a bit.

"So, are we going to talk about your girl?"

He sucked his teeth. "She's not my girl. You are. Stop saying that shit."

"Then what were you doing with her at a bar the other night?"

"Man, I'm so fucking tired of Brian and Denise. I can't ever tell you anything before one of them does."

"True. The bigger question is why you haven't said anything about it and on top of that, you have been ducking me ever since."

"No, I wasn't answering because you lied."

"Okay, Trent. So, what do you have to say about her?"

He told me about her speaking to him at a bar he went to with friends and then left. Apparently, the girl started emailing him last week, but he claimed to have brushed her off. The lunch was supposedly unplanned. They ran into each other again and ended up eating together. In the end, he explained to me who she really was.

Trent apologized about lying before when he cheated with her. All the while, I wanted to hit him in the head with a cast iron pan. This fool was telling me all this so casually as if it was normal to have a fucking meal with someone you fucked around with. Since he had never been this honest before, I listened and kept my mouth closed.

The man swore up and down that nothing was going on and he wouldn't see her again. If they ran into each other, he wouldn't speak from now on. *Sure.*

ƥƥƥ

TODAY WAS MY LAST DAY AT THE OFFICE IN Colorado. The new staff was more than ready. It was bitter-sweet. After all the drama my personal life went through for me to get here, a part of me didn't want to leave. I'd been here about four months.

Trent was Mr. Perfect and had been up here every weekend to prove that he only wanted me. I believed him. He'd be picking me up tonight from the airport.

Mrs. Roland gave me the next two days off, so I had a

four-day weekend to look forward to. Finding a place should be much quicker with my mornings free.

When I landed in Houston, Trent was nowhere to be found. I kept calling him but got nothing. My parents couldn't know about this. They low-key hated him still.

Denise was out of town again. Her grandmother was in the hospital. Brian was the last one on my list. I had to wait a good hour since it was last minute, but he showed up with a smile on his face.

It was nice to see him. I had to tell him about himself after ratting me out to Trent, but he was still family. We stopped by Denny's on the way to my parents' house. It had been so long since we had hung out without the other two. I forgot how funny he was.

It reminded me of college when it was only the two of us before we became a foursome. Trent was on my shit list, but I refused to let him ruin my high of finally being back home. We were there for about an hour before he dropped me off.

My mom was up and waiting on me. It was a little after 9 p.m. They assumed Trent picked me up and I let them. We stayed up until one in the morning doing nothing but talking and laughing. You'd think I'd been overseas for years or something. I saw them a month ago.

♭♭♭

THURSDAY CAME, STILL NO TRENT. MY CAR WAS IN my parents' garage, so I drove to the house. I used my key to get in, but he wasn't there. I was worried. I called his mom and then Brian. No one knew where he was. My first thought was he got hurt in a wreck or something. Why else would he not show up at the airport?

No hospital had admitted him. There were no reported accidents that anyone was seriously hurt in. I started aching on the inside. I sat on the couch thinking of what he could've gotten himself into.

Two hours had passed with no word from him. All of a sudden someone unlocked the front door. Trent walked in with food in his hand.

"What the...Hey, what are you doing here?" he asked. This motherfucker had to be joking. I stood up ready to lose it. "I thought I was picking you up tonight. How'd you get here so fast?" he said with a smirk I could slice off his fucking face.

I recognized this person, but I never thought I'd see him again. This was the same bitch nigga that would play games in the past as if he was clueless. He turned into this character a lot when he was fucking around. Since that bitch was back in the picture, he must've been with her.

Trent walked to me and tried to kiss my lips. All I smelled was the bottles he most definitely had last night or even this morning. It was like he poured it all over his body. There was no way he was sober, and his dumb ass drove here from wherever he was at.

"You've got to be fucking kidding me," I said.

He swiped his hand at me and went to the kitchen.

"What the fuck happened to you, Trent?"

No answer. I wanted to slap that stupid ass look off of his face.

"So, you don't remember that you were supposed to pick me up last night?"

He looked confused, but it wasn't genuine. I wasn't falling for that shit this time.

"Nigga, where were you? I thought something bad happened to you."

"Why are you so loud?" he finally responded.

"What? I'm not loud, dumb ass. You're drunk."

"Yeah, maybe. Last night was the shit. You should've been there."

"Are you fucking serious right now?"

"Stop tripping. You are always tripping over nothing, Kim. You need to relax."

"Look, I don't know what the fuck you're on. Call me when you sober up."

He said something I couldn't hear as I walked out. His car was damn near in the middle of the street. I hoped he'd get a ticket. I called Brian and told him to get his boy. He revealed that Trent had been tripping like this for a while and that he tried to talk some sense into him before.

Apparently, this was the weekday Trent because he was normal with me on the weekends. I couldn't understand why no one told me about it sooner.

Brian claimed he didn't say anything because of how I came down on him about telling my business. This was his way of staying out of it. I wanted to slap him, too.

Trent

Kim and I had a whole month of no arguing, which was a record in the past six months. I only knew because she told me. It sounded ridiculous that she kept tabs on it. Our peaceful record was that short, but things had been good. Well, as good as it could be.

She had me on a tight leash all because I popped a few pills a while ago. It wasn't that big of a deal except that I stood her up at the airport. I was sure she was more pissed at that than the pills.

Kim wouldn't entertain marriage or living together. I wasn't sure, but I had a feeling her family had a lot to do with her change of heart. Not that I'd been Prince Charming or anything. She seemed to be a bit headstrong on the subject and refused to consider it.

We moved her into her new place last night. It was an awkward day since I had to help her dad and brother move her things along with Brian. The same men that came and got all these things from my house were forced to work with me. I could tell they still had a problem, but neither one said anything about it.

They spoke to me and made very little small talk. Most conversations excluded me yet included Brian. Mr. Duncan kept giving me that "I could kick yo' ass" expression whenever I caught him looking my way. I was quiet, kept my distance, and stayed near Kim as much as possible. Not that I was scared, but I wanted him to see that we were good.

The four of them went out to eat and I made an excuse to get out of it. I wasn't sure if everyone knew everything at first, but it became clear that they did.

Whenever I attended their family gatherings, Mrs. Duncan wouldn't look me in the eyes. It's not a fearful avoidance, but one that felt like I didn't even deserve her eye contact.

Hopefully, this treatment will end soon. We were trying to start a new and better life together. By the time we'd walk down the aisle, I wanted to have in-laws that didn't completely hate my guts. Kim acted like it was all in my head. Yeah, right.

Our relationship took a dive after all the recent bullshit and we'd been trying to get it together. Kim thought it would be a good idea to start dating instead of going back to where we were. It was her way of starting over with me.

I understood her motives and could only respect them, but the lack of sex was hard. We couldn't spend the night together. She'd leave my place in the middle of the night to go home to her parents before she moved out again. It drove me a bit crazy to still not get to lay with her at night.

We were once planning to get married and now, nothing. We had sex twice in the past month and that was recent. I didn't know why she took that away from me at a time like this. Kim and I never had an issue in that area. She wanted it as much as I did.

Ever since Toni popped up, Kim seemed to have been holding back. I promised her that I hadn't cheated on her, but maybe she didn't believe me. Or worse, she was getting hers from someone else. Then again, she wasn't that type of woman. If this was punishment, I would have to grin and bear it until she came back around to loving me the way that she did before.

♭♭♭

ANOTHER TWO WEEKS PASSED WITH US HANGING out almost every day, and still no sex. Whenever I tried, she had an excuse about it being that time of the month or she wasn't feeling well enough. She had me worried enough to ask her if she was seeing someone else. Of course, she answered no.

How long were we supposed to go on like this? Things were pretty much getting back to normal.

Kim started hanging out with my mom and sisters again. We had family nights together with them and everything.

Tonight, we had dinner with Brian and Denise at their place. The women cooked for us. They were doing a lot of giggling and whispering in the kitchen. With their open floor plan, it wasn't hard to notice the ladies were up to something.

After dinner, they went back into the kitchen to get our dessert. Denise walked over to the table with a covered silver platter and Kim looked like she was recording us with her phone.

"What is this?" Brian asked Denise. "It's food, crazy," she answered.

"Okay," he said.

"Boy, just open it," Kim rushed to say.

Brian took off the top and there sat a baby food jar of bananas. The both of us were lost. I could see it on his face.

"We're eating baby bananas?" he asked, not really excited about it.

"Look in the lid," Denise told him. She and Kim were giddy, and it was weird as hell.

Brian grabbed a piece of paper from the lid and dropped it. "You lying," he said.

"Nope," she replied through the biggest smile I'd ever seen.

He jumped from his chair. "We're having a baby?" he yelled.

"Yes!" she screamed, hopping a few times.

Brian ran to her, picked her up, and spun her around. I grabbed the paper that was faced down on the table and saw the ultrasound image. Wow.

I walked over to the both of them. "Congratulations!" I hugged Denise and dapped him up.

Kim did the same, but louder. The first thing I thought was that soon enough they'd be so caught up in raising the baby, they wouldn't be in our business. I was indeed happy for them, but more for us.

We left about ten minutes later to let them have time alone. Kim was at their house before I got there so I had to drop her off at home. On the way, she was texting someone and smiling too hard for my comfort.

"What you over there cheesing about?" I asked.

"Nothing. I was telling my mom and them the news about Denise." She put her phone in her purse. "So, what do you think about your best friend becoming a dad soon?" He smile was almost as big as Denise's earlier.

"I'm happy for them. It got me wondering if that would ever be us."

"Why you say that?"

"No reason. It briefly crossed my mind. I mean, it would be nice to have a baby with you."

"Hmph, maybe."

"What's that supposed to mean?" I asked.

"We are still working things out. Babies are not on my mind. We aren't ready."

"Even if we were, it's impossible to make a baby when you never want to do anything with me."

"Really, Trent? That's not true. I thought we were taking things slow."

"But why? We've been together for eight years. What reason do we have to slow down? We've done everything already. Why put it on hold now?"

"I am only trying to protect myself. That's all."

"From what? Me?"

Kim turned away and looked out the window. She didn't answer my question.

"Please tell me this is not about Toni."

"It's not, Trent. It's about you and being able to trust you not to break my heart again. Maybe it is a little about your other woman who you claim to not be involved with."

"So, my word don't mean nothing to you?"

"That's not what I said."

"Well, that's what it sounds like. You think I'm still messing with her. I told you I wasn't, Kim."

"I know. But it's hard to believe. After you told me the whole truth about her, it feels like you have feelings for that woman. I don't want to think that you would lie to me again, but it feels different with you."

"What the hell are you talking about?" I raised my voice.

"Trent, if you are going to start yelling and shit, we need to stop talking. I'm not in the mood to fight with you."

"Babe, I'm sorry. I am only saying that I don't understand."

"Haven't you felt the distance lately?"

"Yeah, but that's because you are putting it there. You won't let me sleep at your place or you at mine. Sex is non-existent. I have been trying to prove myself to you by doing all the things you've asked of me. I don't understand why you are holding out."

"Boy, I am not holding out."

"Then what are you doing? Hell, part of me thinks you're the one fucking someone else."

"What? Don't start that with me again, Trent."

"We both know how you are, so how have you been able to go this long without it. Unless you haven't been," I said.

"First of all, I'm not you. If I wanted to fuck somebody else, I wouldn't be in this relationship. Second, you should know me better than that. Why would I do that to you? I had to deal with you cheating and it wasn't a good feeling. I wouldn't dare do it back to you."

"Well, is it some type of punishment?"

"No, Trent. I guess I want to make sure we are really all in this time."

"Babe, I gave you a ring. I've been all in. You're the one who called everything off," I reminded her, making sure she didn't forget her part in all this.

"You had nothing to do with why I made that decision, right?"

She glared at me, but I kept my eyes on the road and said nothing. I turned on her street and then to her apartment gate. She gave me her gate card to swipe.

"Look, I don't mean for you to think I'm withholding sex to get back at you. I don't want to get fucked over again because this is the last time for us to get it right."

"Kim, I am not doing anything wrong. I promise."

We got to her building. She picked up her purse from the floor and placed it on her lap.

"I want to believe you and I do, mostly. The timing of our struggles and this chick back in the picture has me a little hesitant."

"Damn, Kim. What will it take for you to trust what I've been telling you? She is not back in nothing. I ran into her twice. It was only a coincidence, nothing more. I haven't talked to her since I told you everything."

I could tell she still wasn't convinced. If I knew it would've been this much resistance, I would've never been honest with her. She couldn't handle it and now we were stuck in a sexless, awkward, stagnant state.

🖤🖤🖤

ANOTHER WEEK HAD PASSED BEFORE KIM LET ME IN again. She came to my place after work and finally gave me what I'd been begging for. It lasted only a few minutes. I'd been without feeling her for too many weeks and I couldn't hold it back for long.

After she cleaned herself up, she told me she had to go home. I got up and went to the bathroom expecting to convince her to stay. By the time I came out, she was leaving.

"Kim, wait."

"What's wrong?" she asked, turning from the front door.

"Why are you rushing out? You can stay the night, you know."

"I don't have any clothes here and we both have to go to work in the morning."

"Okay, but you can leave early. I want to lay with you." I really wanted to go for round two. That first one didn't count.

"Leave early?"

"Come on. You can stay one night. Why is it such a big deal anyway? If it's about your family, they don't have to know."

"It's not about them. I told you, I wanted to slow things down."

"But we just…What about one hour? Can you do that much for me?"

"Sure. One hour. Then I'm gone." She put her things

down and we got in the bed. After all of that, I didn't even want to try anything. Kim was acting so different and too determined to "take things slow."

I held her from behind and we lay there quietly. When I started to doze off, her phone alarm went off. She fucking timed it? I got a kiss and she was gone like she said she'd be.

The old me wouldn't take this, but I had no choice. My lady made up her mind and after everything, I had to let her do what she needed to. In the end, I expected us to be on the same page with the same goal: marriage. Kim was a good woman and I didn't want to be the guy that turned her heart. I could have a good life with her and I wanted it.

On the other hand, Toni kept creeping into my mind. The what ifs were getting stronger due to the slow progress with Kim. We had been together so long and had learned how we operate. It was my comfort zone. I didn't know Toni that well besides the sex and a bit of her personality. I liked what I did know but feared what I didn't.

If I broke things off with Kim to go after Toni, would it be worth it? Or could it be worse than what I was currently dealing with? Our relationship used to be predictable, but the uncertainty of Kim's true feelings had me twisted.

♭♭♭

TONIGHT, KIM SPENT TIME WITH HER FAMILY. SHE invited me, but that was the last thing I needed. Mom was out of town visiting my aunt. Otherwise, I'd bother her. I picked up some Chick-fil-a for dinner. On the way back, Brian checked if I was home. He wanted to stop by.

He got to my place about five minutes after I did. The door was unlocked so I wouldn't have to get up when he arrived. He came in, but he wasn't alone. Once Denise stepped inside, I smelled a setup. She went to the bathroom as soon as she got in.

"What the fuck man? Why you didn't tell me she was with you?" I whispered.

"Chill out. She had to use the restroom on our way home. You know how she is about using public ones. She acted like she couldn't wait and asked to stop here since it was on our way home," he whispered back.

"Yeah, whatever. The two of you are always up to something. I am usually the one to pay a price. You better keep her on a leash."

"A leash? Man, if you—"

"Whew! That was close. I thought I wasn't going to make it," Denise said, leaving the bathroom.

"See," Brian said to me. "See what?" she asked.

"Nothing, I was telling him you had to go really bad."

"Oh. What you been up to, Trent?" Denise asked, looking around while standing next to Brian.

"Nothing."

"Mm."

"What's that for?" I asked her.

"Look, I'm not trying to get in your business, but—"

"It's not like it ever stopped you before," I told her.

"Man, chill out," Brian said.

"Nah. The two of you are always in my business. Y'all make things harder than they should be because you can't keep your mouths shut or your opinions to yourselves," I let them know.

"You need to watch your tone with me, Trent. We don't try to make things worse. We have been trying to help you out. Neither of you is ever completely honest with each other but will tell one of us the real deal. It's only fair that the other one knows the truth. That's y'all fault. Even now, there are secrets that we have to hear about. Don't get mad because we care enough to say something," Denise explained.

"What secrets? Ain't nobody got no secrets."

"Oh, so you haven't been emailing that girl, talking about Kim," she said.

What the fuck?

"How the hell would you even know anything like that?"

"How do you think, Trent? The woman you claim to love doesn't trust you and she has good reason not to. Whatever I know, you better believe she is the one who told me."

Fuck! That was why she'd been acting so strange. It had to be the reason. How did Kim see my emails?

Brian pulled her to the side. "What are you doing, Dee?"

"What? He needs to know that he's caught. You know how Kim had been acting lately trying to avoid him and stuff. He needs to know that she knows what he's doing."

"That is not your decision to make, Denise. Why do you keep doing this?" he asked.

"I think it's time for you guys to go. Don't get into no fight over my shit. Go be happy in y'all little world and let me deal with mine," I told them, walking to the door.

Denise tried to keep talking, but Brian stopped her. He apologized for her and they left.

Kim never even hinted anything about this. All that taking it slow bullshit was because she'd been snooping through my stuff. It all made sense. I called her to explain myself and to understand why she went through my emails, but she didn't answer.

I was pissed enough to drive to her apartment, but her car wasn't there. I even drove to her parents' house. This had to be dealt with immediately. She wasn't there either or at least her car wasn't. Knocking on their door was never an option.

On the way home, I tried calling again. This time she

ignored the call and sent it to voicemail. I knew something was up and would find out soon enough.

Nothing was going on with Toni. We were only talking over email, so Kim wouldn't get suspicious. Toni emailed me a few weeks ago and we had been messaging each other. She asked about my day and stuff. I only mentioned the things with Kim once or twice.

There was nothing incriminating about our conversations. If Kim saw all of them, she knew how many times I avoided crossing the line again. Toni wanted more and shared her concern about Kim, but I did nothing but defend Kim. I'm the one who should be mad about all this. Now she was invading my privacy because she won't trust me. Where the fuck was she?

Kim

T RENT KEPT CALLING ME LAST NIGHT. I WASN'T IN the mood. Denise called me and told me what she said to him. I hung up in her face when she tried to explain why she constantly goes behind my back doing these things.

We were all so close and had been for so long that it was beginning to be way too much. I needed space from her. Brian was her accomplice in my mind. I texted her this morning that we needed a break. It felt like I was breaking up with a boyfriend, but it was necessary.

I knew that avoiding Trent forever was impossible. The grown-up thing to do was to face the music and let him get things off his chest. Since he knew about the emails I read, it was too late to come clean organically, which I planned to do at first. This time I'd have to take whatever he dished out because technically I was in the wrong. With good reason, though.

While at work, I texted to meet him for lunch within the next hour. He agreed, and we met at this new burger joint a couple blocks from my job. If we could both be adults and be completely honest, then this conversation wouldn't be as dreadful as I had imagined.

The place was more packed than I expected. They'd better be good. Trent was already in line. I went over to him. We talked about our day so far. I could tell he was pissed. His answers were short.

Another ten minutes passed before we were able to order our food. There weren't any seats left, so we went to his car to eat.

When we got in, neither of us touched the food. It smelled great, but my stomach was ready to get this conversation over with.

"So, are you going to say anything?" he asked. "I was waiting on you."

"Fine, why did you go through my emails?"

"I saw an email notification pop up on your phone with her name on it."

"That's it. You were doing all of this over one email that you didn't even read?"

"Well, to be honest, I did read it. I read all of them when I used your laptop one day."

He exhaled hard. It seemed like he was letting out air for minutes and not seconds. "Why didn't you ask me about it?"

"Because I didn't believe that you'd tell me the whole truth if I did. I wanted to see it for myself. After reading it once, I went back to see more of the conversation up to the last time I was at your place."

"Did you find what you were looking for?" he asked, coldly.

Whenever he didn't show his emotions immediately, the eruption would come out later and most likely at the wrong time.

"Yeah, enough to know that you lied to me about talking

to her. On top of that, you talk to her about me. I'm not cool with that."

"I'm not cool with my woman going through my shit."

"If you would be one hundred with me, I wouldn't have to. I knew you were lying the whole time. All I needed was proof and that's what I found."

"So, me having a conversation is proof of what?"

"Of you cheating emotionally."

He looked at me sideways. "What the hell are you talking about?"

"Trent, you are letting her into your personal life. Asking for advice about how to deal with me not fucking you. I saw what that bitch said about me."

"That means you also saw me shut that down, right? If you saw everything, you saw that too."

"Okay, but you shouldn't even be entertaining this girl in the first place. What the fuck is wrong with you? You cheated on me with her, why are you talking to her in any form? I don't give a damn what the conversation is about. There shouldn't be a fucking conversation."

My heart was pushing through my chest. It was getting to me and the last thing I wanted to do was cry in front of him over this.

All the shit from this year alone was enough to end us and now he was buddies with the one person that should be off-limits. I would never do that to him. It was fucked up.

It was quiet for a couple minutes and I felt myself about to lose it. He wasn't getting it, acting like what he did was normal. He knew better, which is why he lied about it. I needed to get out of this car. I felt like punching him in his throat.

"I gotta get back to work. Are we done? You ain't saying nothing so I assume we are, right?"

"Kim, I'm sorry. I didn't think it would be a big deal since

I'm not doing anything with her. We were only talking inno-cently. I don't like that you were snooping through my stuff, but I understand that I was wrong in how I handled this."

Who the hell was this guy?

"I'm sorry too. I should've come to you about it instead of going behind your back," I told him.

"So, are we good? I promise, I will cut everything off with her, so you won't have to wonder about anything. Okay?"

"Okay."

He leaned over and kissed me before I got out and went to my car. I drove back to work and ate my food in the parking lot.

♥♥♥

WHEN I GOT HOME, TRENT WAS PARKED NEAR MY apartment. I didn't remember him telling me he was coming over. I pulled into my garage and met him on the sidewalk.

"Hey. What are you doing here?" I asked.

"I had time to think after our talk and wanted to reassure you that I only want you. I don't know why I was talking to Toni behind your back or at all. She was an ear when I couldn't talk to you and now I see how that's fucked up."

"Okay."

"Can I come inside?" He had some bags in his hand. I saw Red Lobster in one and H-E-B in the other.

"Uh, sure."

We walked to my apartment and went inside. He went to the kitchen and sat everything on the counter. I changed my clothes in my bedroom.

"What are you doing?" I asked, walking into the kitchen.

"I'm making dinner. An apology dinner. I got some red and white wine. Do you have some candles or something you can put on the table?"

"Not any we wouldn't taste. All of them are scented."

"Never mind then."

"Excuse me, sir. Where is my boyfriend? What have you done with him?"

He laughed. "Whatever. You wanted different; I'm trying different."

"Okay, then I will shut up and let you do your thing."

"Could you get some wine glasses?"

"Of course."

Trent's newfound behavior was weird in a good way. Trent had not one romantic bone in his body unless he was in trouble. Even then, he never did this for me. It felt nice and was the first glimpse that we could move forward and be better.

I sat the glasses on the table. Trent pulled a chair out for me. "You are going all out, huh?"

"Hey, a man's gotta do what's necessary to keep his lady happy."

I gently knocked on his forehead. "Seriously, Trent are you in there?"

"You ain't funny. I'm right here in front of you.

So, take it all in."

Something about the way he said that made me want to skip dinner. Besides, he owed me for those three pumps I got the last time we made love.

He went to the kitchen and I followed him. Once he grabbed the wine from the fridge, I took it from him and put it on the counter.

"What are you doing?" he asked. "Nothing."

I kissed him but kept my eyes open to see if his were closed. They were. Whenever he enjoyed anything, he would close his eyes. It made me kiss him harder. When he moaned, I knew I had him.

Trent grabbed my ass and pulled me closer to him. I bit his bottom lip and pulled it a little. Then I unbuckled his belt and unbuttoned his jeans. I put my hand in and grabbed the very thing that kept poking my thigh.

"Damn, babe. Whatchu tryna do?" he asked, because I was stroking his shaft with a tight grip.

"A girl's gotta do what's necessary to make her man happy."

He let out the sexiest laugh. "See, you playing."

Trent picked me up with my legs around his waist and walked us to my bed. After he laid me down, he stood over me and took his shirt off. I lay my head back and put by feet on his chest. I slid them down to his stomach and then pulled his pants down with them.

He got on top of me and kissed my lips softly, before sliding his tongue into my mouth. I inhaled him and felt calm. I slid my hands into his boxers and grabbed his ass. Then he broke from my lips and pulled my shirt over my head. After my bra came off, he stared at me for a few moments. I didn't know what he was thinking, but it felt nice to be gazed upon and not glared at.

I took the rest of my clothes off with his help. Once I lay back again, he kissed my breasts and soon after his tongue came out to play. He knew that drove me crazy. I started moving my hips from side to side enjoying every second.

While still working on my top half, his fingers made their way to that throbbing spot in between my legs. He played with it enough to make me lose it. I made him stop because the only thing to top that feeling was to have all of him.

"Do you have any condoms?" he asked. "No, don't you?"

"Nah, we used the last one last time. I forgot to get more. Why don't you have any?"

"Because you always had them."

"Shit," he said.

I put my hand on my forehead. I couldn't believe he came here unprepared.

"Okay, what if I pull out right when I feel it coming?"

"Hell, no. I am not trying to get pregnant by you right now."

"Why you say it like that? It's not like it would be the end of the world."

"Ugh, get up. We are not doing this."

"Babe, stop. We can get started a little bit and be okay. Come on," he said, whining.

I couldn't help but laugh. He looked so pitiful. "Hell to the hell naw, naw, naw."

He kissed me again, but it still wasn't going to change my mind. He went down to my neck, then my breasts, to my navel, until he got low enough to bite my inner thigh.

"Trent, stop. We can't."

"I'm not doing anything," he said, teasing. Then his teeth were gently pulling on that spot again. I tried to move away, but he had me trapped with how he was holding me. I moaned as he sucked it and flickered his tongue. It went on for minutes until I came.

"That's not fair," I told him.

"What's not? Are you not pleased?" he asked, with a seductive look.

"Oh, you want to play, huh?"

"I don't know what you're talking about."

I grabbed his dick and squeezed it, but not too hard. He moaned. I kept rubbing it up and down until we switched positions and he was on his back.

I straddled one of his thighs as I went faster and faster. He would thrust upward every now and then, so I went even faster and held it tighter. I knew he was getting close, so I kissed the tip with a little tongue. Seconds later, he exploded.

"Fuck!" he yelled.

I wanted more. It wouldn't happen unless one of us went to the store. By one of us, I meant him. The way he looked right now, he wasn't going anywhere. We lay there next to each other for a few minutes until he started snoring in my ear.

I got out of bed and warmed up my plate of food and put his away. After I finished eating, I watched TV until I fell asleep on the couch.

The phone rang and woke me up. It was after two a.m. I went to the kitchen where it was, but it wasn't my phone. Because it said unknown on the caller ID, I couldn't help myself.

I answered it with a grunt, in case the person was calling for Trent. It could've been the wrong number.

"Hey, Trent. You up? I didn't want to call earlier in case you weren't alone," a woman said.

I gripped the phone tighter. "So, you must be Toni."

"Um, I think I have the wrong number."

"Yeah, right. You know damn well you got the right number, but you definitely got the wrong one."

"Look, Kim. I don't want no problems."

"Oh, so now you gonna act like you know me. Don't fucking call this number again," I yelled.

I tapped the "end call" button so hard that I hurt my damn finger. Trent rushed out of my bedroom in his underwear. I threw his phone at him. "Ouch. What the hell?"

"Why the fuck is the woman you swore you wouldn't talk to anymore calling you? And this fucking late? Is this your usual time?"

"Wait, babe. I can explain. It's not what you think."

"It's never what I think until it's proven to be exactly what I knew it was all along. You've been fucking her, haven't you?"

"Kim, don't do this. I told you I didn't do anything with her. We were having a good night. Let's not ruin it."

"Nigga, didn't you hear what I said? Your little girlfriend called your phone. You told me you never gave her your number and it was all email."

"But that was earlier today. I didn't have time to tell her not to call...I mean—"

"You son of a bitch! You just admitted it. How long have you been talking to her on the phone?"

"Dammit! Why do we always have to end up here? You keep asking me the same shit and I keep giving the same answer. When will you believe me?"

"When you tell the whole fucking truth for once. Matter of fact, I don't even want to know. You need to leave. Now!"

Trent stood still for a minute before he got dressed. There was nothing he could do or say at this point. Fuck him forever.

"Kim," he said after he put his shoes on.

"Nope. Get out."

"Listen. Please," he yelled.

"Go talk to your hoe," I told him, walking to the door.

I opened it, so his ass could get the fuck out. To think I actually believed his bitch ass earlier.

Trent walked toward me and looked at me like he thought he could change my mind. So, I helped him out with a nudge. "Go, Trenton."

Once he was on the other side, I closed and locked the door.

ᛗᛗᛗ

A WEEK HAD PASSED WITH NO RUN-INS WITH TRENT. Every call was blocked, texts deleted, and pop-ups ignored. He came to my door at least four times while I was home. I turned my TV up as loud as I could to block him trying to talk to me through the door. I didn't care anymore. It was officially over for me.

Denise and Brian were also blocked in case he got to them. I needed to be alone and free of all their nonsense. Everyone was getting on my nerves.

I requested a week off from work and took a trip to visit my aunt in Muir Beach, California. It was everything I wanted to be: peaceful.

Aunt Vivica was my dad's sister and they acted so much alike. She wasn't an all up in your business type of person. If I said everything was good, she accepted it. This time, I told her what had been going on. Her only advice was to do what made me happy.

My aunt had a gorgeous house that was left to her by her late husband, so it was only the two of us there. The views were breathtaking. I spent most of my first day on her balcony. I couldn't break away from it.

Every meal was eaten at her outdoor dining table. No wonder she won't move back home like my dad had been begging her to do for over fifteen years. Who would ever want to leave this place?

We went shopping and sightseeing. She took me to Napa Valley for one night and then Catalina Island for two nights. I couldn't remember what her husband did for a living, but he was a wealthy man and made her a wealthy widow. The two of them had a real love. It showed every time they came to visit us back home in the past.

I was so happy for her because her first husband was like Trent in his ways and didn't treat my aunt the way she deserved. Her late husband came into the picture and swept her off her feet. Good thing he was a great guy instead of another rich asshole.

She treated me to every luxury she could think of. I appreciated every single moment. On the last night, she almost convinced me to move there. Even though it was tempting, I didn't want to leave my parents. Colorado revealed that to me. As much as I complained about my mom, being so far from her didn't feel that great. We sipped wine by the moonlight and took in the peace of nature.

My aunt wasn't preachy, but the stories about her first husband taught me a lesson. They got married after dating for six years. She felt like she wasn't getting any younger and they had my cousin. She knew he wasn't her perfect match, but life happened to them and they settled with each other.

After marriage, they had one more kid together. Her ex-husband had three more with three different women before she finally left him. I'd be damned if I allowed Trent to do that to me.

Getting out now would save both of us time and frustration. I refused to live a lifetime of misery, infidelity, and insecurity with him. That was the only future I could imagine having if I became his wife.

Trent

I GAVE EVERYTHING I COULD TO REACH KIM AND clear shit up. If she thought I would wait forever, she had another thing coming. All the fucks I could give were used up last week. I tried and failed. My assumption was that we were over, and I could do whatever I wanted with whomever.

Brian would call to check on me acting like he didn't know what was up. That shit irritated me. There was no way Kim hadn't told one or both her jaded side of the story. I knew they ate up every word. I told him I was good and that I didn't need to be checked on like no damn child.

I started hanging out with my other friends. The ones that knew how to have a good time. And a good time was what we had every night. I didn't know there was a club poppin' every day of the week. I was glad they did.

Every single night this week, I met the guys at a new spot. Then I left with a woman on my arm. It didn't take much, and they were only in it for the sex. What more could a man ask for?

I didn't have to play games with these women. We did our thing and they called a cab or someone to pick them up.

The first night, I had a feeling I was going to get an invoice. She was too eager. It turned out, she was getting married soon and wanted to get her cravings out of her system. If she wanted to fuck random dudes until her wedding night, why get married?

The others were equally eager and talked less. Some of the time, we'd find a stall in the club and do it there instead of leaving together. It was all good with me. I had never been so satisfied in my life.

The freedom was reviving, and I didn't have to hear anyone bitching about it. This was the life I was meant to have. I couldn't come up with one reason why I should ever give this up again.

After the first week, I ventured out on my own. It wasn't every night but at least three or four. I made sure to be careful with protection and to be clear that I wasn't trying to pay for sex when a woman came on too strong. Some of the women who approached me were escorts. As soon as I said I wasn't paying, they walked away.

It had been about eight women in the last two weeks. They were down to do anything and showed me some tricks I didn't know were a thing. My sex life had been lacking big time even when we were at it on a regular.

♭♭♭

KIM HADN'T CONTACTED ME IN THREE WEEKS. I hoped she was okay, but that's all. Toni emailed me apologizing about the night Kim answered the phone. She hoped she didn't cause any trouble. I told her that everything was cool and that it was safe to call me whenever. I had to let Toni know that I wasn't going to jump into another relationship even though she wanted to. So, we stayed friends, nothing more.

One night out with the guys, we went to a bar to play pool. Some woman in the corner was watching me. Even when I looked her way, she didn't back down. She was with a group of women that were younger than us but old enough to be in here. After a while, it was her turn to play. She kept bending over the pool table making sure I saw her.

One game later, her group was leaving. We made eye contact and she waved for me to come over. She told me her name was Shaunie and gave me her number. It was too easy.

It almost seemed like I had a sign somewhere telling the world I was a free man. I'd never gotten so much attention before Kim. Then again, I was a youngin' when we started dating. Over the years, the cloud of misery must have hung over my head and scared women off. It felt good to be seen again.

A few days later, I called Shaunie and we planned a late dinner. The first thing I made sure she knew was that I wasn't looking for a relationship. Neither was she. I couldn't wait to take her down. Her body was shaped like Toni's, but she had Kim's beauty. They didn't look alike or anything, but for some reason, she reminded me of a young Kim. I didn't notice it until we had dinner.

I learned that she was a bartender and in college. She was barely twenty-one. I was only twenty-eight but still felt old as hell with her. The first night ended with us in my bed. She had a little too much energy. We had sex at least three times. Granted it was great, but she wore my ass out.

Tonight, I met her at the restaurant she worked at. I sat at the bar with a couple of her friends. They were flirting with me hard right in front of her. One of them asked if we were down for a threesome.

I looked at Shaunie and she answered the woman by kissing her over the counter. The woman put her hand on my dick and laughed because it was getting hard. Shaunie told her to meet us at her place around midnight. I guess it was going down.

On her break, she came and sat on my lap. She asked me if I had ever had a threesome before. I lied and told her once. Then she explained to me that she used to date the girl we were going to meet later so they may have a go-around before I get to join them. I was ready to go right then. She kissed me as if no one else was there. Shaunie was so young and free. I loved it.

When we came up for air, Brian walked in. I saw him, and he saw me. Shaunie's break had ended and as she walked away, I smacked her ass.

One of the bartenders gave him a beer. I walked over to him. "You stalking me or something?"

He sucked his teeth. "My wife wanted some wings from this place. I had no idea I'd run into you with your...whatever she is to you."

"It's none of your business or anyone else's you decide to run your mouth to."

"My nigga, I didn't come here for you. You can go back to where you were."

"Looks like someone grew his own set of balls. Good for you."

"Fuck you." The bartender handed him a bag of food.

"Yeah, whatever. Be a good boy and go home to your pregnant wife."

"Don't get mad that you don't have what I have. You wouldn't know what to do with a good woman. You already proved that."

"You right. I'd rather keep my nuts and be a real man and not my woman's bitch. I hope you don't have a boy. Wouldn't want him to grow up being some soft ass nigga like his daddy."

"What the fuck you say? You lowlife, cheating asshole. How can you talk shit about my kid? At least I'll have one. No wonder Kim had a miscarriage. The baby must've known what kind of fuck up he would've had for a father."

My chest hardened. Brian turned to walk away. I grabbed him and then felt my face hit a fucking wall.

When I opened my eyes, people were standing over me. Shaunie looked scared.

"Are you okay?" she asked.

I stumbled when I stood. "What happened?"

"You tell me. You were going back and forth with some guy, then he punched you in the face."

"Somebody punched me?"

"Yeah. He hit you and walked away as if nothing happened. Did you know him?"

Brian hit me? What the fuck? I was a little out of it.

"Yeah, he was an old friend."

"Oh. Well, it looks like you ain't friends no more."

"Damn, how long was I out?"

"Less than a minute."

"That muthafucka."

The conversation had hit me harder than the punch. Kim had a miscarriage? "Um, I have to go."

"Okay. Are you still down for tonight with my girl?"

I forgot about that already. "Can I get a rain check? I need to go handle something."

"Sure. Be careful if you are going after that dude."

I laughed, and it hurt. I got out of there fast and probably won't go back. I didn't want to be known as the guy that got knocked out. It was embarrassing enough for it to happen in front of Shaunie.

A miscarriage? I tried to think of a time when this could have happened. Was he lying? Was this recent? When the hell was she pregnant? My head started spinning, and I didn't drink much. Kim wouldn't answer her phone.

I was near her parents' house and decided to drive by to see if she was there before going to her apartment. I was so glad I did because her car was outside and so was she. I saw her parents, Keisha, and Kendrick with a couple other people.

I parked across the street and walked over to them. "Kim?" I yelled to get her attention without running up on her.

"Trent? What are you doing here?"

"I need to talk to you."

"Can we not do this right now?"

"Is everything okay, baby girl?" Mr. Duncan asked. "Yes, Daddy."

"Mr. Duncan. I don't mean to pop up on you guys, but this is urgent."

Kim walked closer to me. "What happened to your eye? Were you fighting?"

"Brian hit me."

"Brian?"

"Yeah, it was right after he told me you had a miscarriage with my baby"

I heard a few gasps and realized I wasn't the only one she kept this from. It didn't even matter, I should've been the first to know.

"Miscarriage? You were pregnant?" Mrs. Duncan asked Kim.

She didn't answer.

"So, it's true," I said.

"Trent, you need to leave," her dad told me while comforting his wife.

"No, I'm not going until she tells me the truth."

"What is he talking about, Kim?" her sister asked. Kim started crying. It still hurt to see her tears, but I was more hurt that she had my baby inside her and never told me about it. "When did this happen, Kim?" I asked.

She looked up at me, then to everyone else. "Look, I didn't say nothing to any of you about it because I didn't want you to look at me how you are now."

Her mother burst into tears. Mr. Duncan was still holding her.

"Mom, don't cry. I'm okay. I didn't want to worry you," she said.

"Kim, when did this happen?" I asked again.

"A couple months before you proposed," she finally admitted.

I felt sick. In my mind, I thought it was from the last time we had sex, which was a little over a month ago. To think that she kept this from me for over half a year and Brian knew about it. Why the fuck did he know about my baby and I didn't?

"Why didn't you tell me?" I asked.

"I can't talk about this right now. I have to go. Mom, everybody, I'm sorry," she said through her tears.

"Wait," I yelled to stop her from leaving.

She got in her car and drove away. I followed her home. Another night could not go by without her telling me everything.

Kim managed to make it to her place a few minutes before me. I kept getting caught up at red lights behind her.

Someone was leaving when I pulled up, so I drove through the exit gate. When I found a spot, she was barely making it out of her garage. I ran to her and grabbed her, so she couldn't run away. It looked like she'd been crying the whole time.

"Tell me what happened, Kim. Why would you keep something like that from me?"

"I didn't want to hurt you."

"Hurt me how?"

"Who wants to say 'hey, I was pregnant, but not anymore'? It happened so fast."

"But when you first found out, why didn't you tell me?"

"That was the same time you got mad at me for not coming to your place in the middle of the night. You were drunk, so I don't know if you remember. But earlier that day was when I took the home test. I was waiting to tell you in person, but we fell out. The next day I confirmed it with my doctor. I was about seven weeks. A week later, I went to the emergency room for really bad cramps and bleeding. The baby was gone."

We were still standing by her car. "How did Brian know?"

"Denise went with me to the doctor both times. I didn't know he knew until later. I made them promise not to tell you. It didn't seem necessary."

"That wasn't your decision to make, Kim. Dammit! Why do you always think your way is the only way? You should've told me."

"Why? It wouldn't have changed anything."

"You don't know that." I raised my voice. I tried to stay calm after noticing her fidget with her keys. "Why didn't you tell your family?"

"Who wants to tell my mom about an unplanned pregnancy with a boyfriend? I would have come clean, but the baby was gone as quickly as she came."

"She?"

"I don't know. He. It doesn't matter now. My family wasn't supposed to ever know."

"Well, lies always come to light some way," I said. "Yeah, you should know that better than anybody."

As much as I wanted to hate her for keeping a secret like this, I couldn't. She had no control of the baby not making it. Plus, it seemed to be a soft spot for her. She wasn't much of a crier.

We walked to her apartment. I went inside to make sure she was okay. An hour ago, I was ready to let her have it. Seeing her after so long and knowing how hurt she was over it made it hard to stay angry.

Kim gave me an unopened bag of frozen chopped bell peppers for my eye. I haven't seen it yet, but she said it looked bad. I told her how I got the black eye and she laughed. Neither of us could believe how Brian came at me about this. His words hurt about as much as my eye did.

We talked about the baby and even though she was calm, tears kept falling. She apologized for not telling me because she thought she was doing the right thing. Keeping it from her judgmental family was understandable, but it sucked that she went through that without me. I felt bad for everything following that time.

I knew that things were over between us, but I wanted to be here for her now since she didn't give me the chance to do so when it happened. I held her in my arms and she cried for our baby.

When she fell asleep, I put her on her bed. I wouldn't be able to lock the door if I left, so I slept on the couch.

The next morning, she got up and made breakfast. We ate and then I went home. I talked to my mom about it and found out that she experienced a miscarriage before she got pregnant with me. It was a painful time for her too.

My mom always knew what to say in every situation I had with Kim. It was like they were the same. She understood all that Kim was and everything she did. Nothing I told her came to much surprise. Of course, she was sad that she lost a grand-child but even more about Kim basically going through that alone.

I saw things differently in how the end of us played out. There was no turning back, but I had so many regrets. Neither one of us was perfect. Being that she kept giving me chances throughout the years proved she did love me more than I gave her credit for. I didn't always agree with her choices, but now I understood why she made some of them.

If only she was this open and honest when we had a fighting chance.

Kim

MOM WOULDN'T TAKE ANY OF MY CALLS. EVEN WHEN I tried to use my dad to get her to talk to me, she refused. Dad told me she'd be home alone this evening because he was going bowling with my brother. Friday Father Night is what they called this corny, but cute tradition.

Everyone else had sympathy and supported me. Daddy called me daily to ask how I was doing since the news broke. It wasn't new to me, but he said he wanted to make up for not being there when I needed him. I made sure he knew that I didn't hold anything against him. It was my decision to keep things under wraps and he had nothing to be sorry for.

After work, I drove straight to my parents' house. My dad was on his way out when I arrived. He gave me a hug and wished me luck. My mom was a major handful when she wanted to be. I walked into the house and found her in the kitchen washing dishes.

"Hey, Mom."

"Kimberly," she said, never turning to look at me.

I sat at the kitchen table waiting for her to finish. Her being upset over my miscarriage was confusing. Yes, she may be disappointed in me for keeping it a secret, but anger was not an emotion I expected from her.

"Do you need help with anything?" I asked to pass the time until we could sit and talk. She didn't answer. I scrolled through my phone in silence.

When she finished, she walked to the back of the house. I assumed she was going to come back. Five minutes later, it was clear she was ignoring me. That woman could be so childish at times. I walked to her room's door and knocked. She still didn't say anything.

"Mom, could you please talk to me?"

"For what? So, you can lie."

"I didn't lie about anything. It wasn't something I wanted to share with everyone at the time."

"Even your own mother, Kim? How could you not tell me about you being pregnant?" The door swung open. "How could you be so careless and get pregnant in the first place?"

"It's not like I tried to. I don't even remember how it happened. It just did."

She sat on her bed. I sat in her reading chair in the corner. "Mom, why are you so mad about this?"

"Because you should've said something. You knew better. You were ashamed, weren't you?"

"I don't know. Maybe. I was more heartbroken than anything else. I was mad at myself for getting pregnant, then I lost it. I never had a chance to get excited before it was all over."

"Excited? For what? To have a bastard child with the worst person you could choose?"

"Whoa, whoa. That's a bit harsh."

"You were about to throw your future away for someone who was never good enough for you."

"So, having us ruined your life?"

"Oh, no. We are not the same. Your father and I truly

loved each other and were married before you came into the picture. We were prepared for a family. You were being reckless."

Where was all of this coming from? Is that what she really thought of me? My face suddenly moistened with tears.

"I never knew I was such a disappointment to you, Mom. You need to understand that it was a difficult time for me. You see why I didn't tell you? Look how you are acting right now."

"Please. You didn't say anything because you knew it was the biggest mistake of your life. That miscarriage saved you a lifetime of pain."

That did it. I said nothing else and walked out. I vowed to never step foot in her house again. My mother had her ways, but I would not stand for this cruelty.

When I got to my car, I called my dad in tears and told him what happened. He told me to stay and wait for him. I couldn't.

ᛒᛒᛒ

Saturday morning came, and I stayed in bed all day. My head hurt from all the crying. Denise, my dad, and my sister called me. I didn't answer either of them. It wasn't a good time. Denise kept texting me apologizing for Brian. I didn't care anymore.

All the two of them did was apologize for butting their noses where they didn't belong. The only reason we started talking again was because she asked me to pray for her grandmother who was in the hospital. She flew out to Georgia yesterday to be with her family.

I got out of bed a little after five p.m., starving. My kitchen was bare. I usually went grocery shopping on Friday's after work. That's what I should've done instead of going to my mom. Now, I had nothing to eat but one egg, a few canned goods, and crackers.

I searched for any place that would deliver anything besides pizza and found a Chinese restaurant. While ordering, they said it would be almost an hour until I'd get my food. So, I took a long, hot shower. When I put on pajamas, I remembered that Trent left vodka in the freezer a while ago and I still never opened those bottles of wine.

Shots weren't really my thing and I had nothing to mix it with, so wine it was. I tried repeatedly and failed to get the damn cork open without a corkscrew. Vodka would have to do.

I poured some into a glass and sipped it. I gagged. How could anyone drink this straight? Something had to be in the kitchen that could help this taste better.

There were a few juice boxes left from when Keisha and Tina came over with my nephews a couple weeks ago. I cut a hole in the fruit punch box and squeezed it into my glass. It still tasted horrible, but no gagging.

I finished the whole glass and made a second one by the time my food came. The guy was rude and ten minutes past an hour. I gave him a quarter tip and slammed the door in his face. The food wasn't the best, but I was too hungry to complain. While eating, I texted everyone who called me earlier to let them know I was okay.

Denise kept calling me since this morning. I accepted her apology already and didn't know why she needed to talk to me so bad. I texted if her grandmother was okay to see if that's why she was trying to reach me. She let me know that her grandmother was still alive but getting worse. I told her I'd say a prayer for her family but couldn't talk. Not sure how much help I'd be.

Denise claimed she wanted to make sure I was okay after everything with Brian and Trent. She knew Trent confronted me with my family present, but not about my mom's behavior last night. I lied about being good and that was the end of it.

I turned on a marathon about women snapping and killing their husbands or boyfriends. After a couple of hours, I finished the bottle, my food, and learned a few ways to get away with murder. Well, almost. The women they talked about were caught.

Another episode began and minutes later it sounded like the police at my door. I rushed and opened it to find Brian standing there. Denise does not listen.

"What are you doing here?"

"I'm trying to check on you."

"Brian, I told your wife that I was okay. There is no need for your babysitting services. You can go back home."

More would've been said, but my head started spinning. I felt the doorway catch my fall.

"Damn, girl. What are you doing to yourself?" he asked, helping me stand.

We walked to the couch. Well, Brian did most of the walking. I felt like I was floating.

"Ugh, you've been drinking."

"Oh, shut up. People can drink. We can't all be so perfect like you and your wife. Everyone else has real problems."

"We're not perfect. You don't have to do this to yourself. You're better than this."

"Better than what?" I asked and sat up straight or at least I tried to. "Am I better than that asshole that *you* introduced me to? This is your fault. I wish I never met him."

"Kim, stop this." He sat next to me on the couch judging me like he was innocent.

"You should've stopped yourself," I said feeling the tears start up again. "Trent didn't need to know I was ever pregnant. But ol' righteous Brian had to tell him. What were you thinking? Now my whole family knows, and my mom fucking hates me."

"I was trying to help you. I wanted him to know what he had and what he would miss out on."

"What do you care?" I tried to get up and fell right back down to the couch.

"I care, Kim. Always have. Even right now, I care enough to make sure you don't hurt yourself. Denise is worried and wants to get a morning flight back here because of you. We all care about you."

"Aww, that's so sweet." I tapped his cheek a couple of times. He grabbed my hand to stop me.

My phone rang, but I couldn't get to it. Brian made it in time and answered it.

"Don't be answering my phone. Give it to me."

"Yeah, I think she'll be fine. She's a bit drunk. I'll sleep over, so you won't have to worry," he said to the other person on the phone.

"Who is that? Give me my phone."

Brian walked further away, so I couldn't really understand what he was saying. I assumed it was Denise since he was still talking.

I lay my head back and stared at the ceiling. Tears started rolling down my neck. My life was taking a turn that I wasn't prepared for. Trent screwed me over and now I had to face everyone else like I did something wrong after losing a baby.

Brian came back to the couch with a bottle of water. I rolled my eyes and looked away. He pulled me up so that I could sit straight, opened the bottle, and put it in my hands.

"Drink it."

"You don't tell me what to do."

"Drink the water, Kim!"

"Stop yelling at me. I'm not in the mood to fight anymore.

I've fought everyone I loved and who I thought loved me. I'm tired of it."

"All I'm trying to do is help you."

"You helped plenty already. Your help is too dangerous."

He put his hand on his face and let out a sigh. "If you only knew."

"Only knew what?"

"You think I wanted to tell you about Trent with those girls back then or even now? You think I wanted to hurt you like that? Then to let out the secret that you should have never kept to prove a point to him and set him straight. I was doing it for you. I love you too much to see you get treated like that. If I didn't help, you would've gotten back with his bum ass. You keep trying to make a life with someone that wasn't for you in the first place."

"What the hell are you talking about? How you know what life I'm supposed to have?"

"Because it should've been me," he yelled, before standing up.

I almost sobered up. He scared me.

"You keep acting like you don't know why shit ain't working with him. It's because he wasn't meant for you. How can you not see that all this time?"

"How was I supposed to know things would be like this?"

"I could've told you from the start."

"Whatever."

"It's not whatever. I was right there in front of you the whole time. As soon as some guy who dresses like he owns the world and acts like he's God's gift to women showed up, you got blindsided. All you saw was the physical and tried to make a life based on that alone."

I was speechless.

"He showed you over and over what kind of dude he was. But no, you had to have him over me."

"Wait, what?" I shook my head rapidly. My ears were tripping. Damn that vodka.

"Nothing, Kim."

"Why are you acting like this?"

"Because I wanted you and you knew it. But you chose the asshole and pushed me off on your best friend."

My jaw dropped. "Okay, hold up. That is not how it happened. You told me you only wanted to be friends."

"It was too late by then." Brian got up and sat on the chair furthest from me.

"No, it wasn't. I chose you and you rejected me. I remember that night like it was yesterday. You pushed me away."

"You were already with him and I was with Denise. It was wrong."

"Everything after that night was wrong. You broke my heart first, Brian. So, yeah I stayed with Trent all this time because I didn't know what else to do."

I got up and went to the bathroom. This conversation was not happening. I never wanted to go back to that time. I wet a towel with hot water, held it on my face, and leaned against the wall. My head hurt and my heart raced. Everything up to now felt like a huge disappointment and waste of my time. The towel was still on my face as I slid down.

Brian knocked on the door. I didn't want to face him. "Go home. I don't want you here."

That one night in college was so clear. We had finished our finals for the semester. Trent and Denise were both busy and couldn't join us for drinks. Brian's roommate was twenty-one and had the kitchen stocked with liquor. He had already left for the summer, but he didn't take the bottles.

Being only twenty ourselves, we never had access to that much alcohol. We overdid it. One thing led to another and we were naked. I had never been so gone in my life. It was like an outer body experience. That was when I knew that I wanted to be with him. The next morning, he said we'd made a big mistake and he swore off alcohol.

All this time I thought he'd forgotten about it. I tried to. We were all too close. A week didn't go by without me having to see him with Denise. I loved her, and I was happy that she got the best man. He was too good for me. So, we stayed really good friends and acted like none of it ever happened. It would destroy so much if anyone else knew about it.

"I'm coming in," he said from the other side of the door.

"No," I told him, but he walked in anyway. Damn. I thought I locked it. I couldn't look at him.

"Kim, I'm sorry for all of that in there. I—"

"It's okay. I made you upset. I know you didn't mean any of it."

He cleared his throat and sat down next to me. "You have no idea how much I meant every word."

"What?"

"Look, I know this is the worst thing I could say to you right now. But it's been hanging over my head ever since that night. I love you. I've always been in love with you."

"No, Brian. You don't know what you are saying. I blame myself. You guys are too involved with my bullshit. You are confused because you feel sorry for me, but I'm okay. Well, I will be."

"I know exactly what I'm saying."

"You are married to my best friend. We cannot be having this—"

His lips were touching mine. It was so wrong, and I tried to pull away, but I couldn't. Nothing was listening to my brain. Not my heart or my body.

We sat there kissing each other slowly as if time had stopped for our lips to feel each other one more time. I put my hand on his face and breathed him in. Our kiss started to taste like my tears. All of a sudden, I realized what I was doing to Denise and got up.

"No, no, no. We can't do this," I said.

He stood up and straightened his shirt. "Shit, you're right. I'm sorry."

"Um, you should go."

"Yeah."

We left the bathroom and I walked him to the door. He opened it and left. On my way to the kitchen, the wall caught my fall. Only this time, I was completely in my right mind.

"What the fuck are you doing, Kim?" I said out loud.

Knowing Brian, he would have to tell Denise and I would end up losing my best friend forever.

Someone knocked at my door. At this time of night, it must've been him. Right then, I saw his keys on the table. I grabbed them and took them to the door.

"You forgot these?"

"Um, yeah. Can't go anywhere without those."

We laughed a little. I was relieved that we didn't fuck up everything even further. I handed him the keys. When he got them, our hands touched. I felt something on the inside.

"Ok, so. I will see you around."

"Kim? Do you..." He looked both ways for some reason.

"Do I what?"

"Man, fuck it," he said as he pushed his way into my apartment.

Brian grabbed my waist and pulled me into him. He kissed me hard like he meant it. I couldn't deny him or myself anymore. I wanted him. Nothing else mattered.

He picked me up and walked to the couch. My body was acting on its own. He laid me down and got on top of me. His lips never broke from mine since we started. Our tongues met again and took me back to that night. Only this time, the stakes were higher.

Brian

As I lay on top of Kim, all I saw was her eyes. They told me everything I needed to hear with no words spoken. Her lips felt like they missed mine. She looked into my eyes and I let her gaze until she relaxed.

There was no doubt on my part and I wanted this to be all that I had dreamed of. Many nights went by with the feeling I remembered from our first time. Never did I believe I'd have this opportunity again. It wouldn't be wasted on hesitation and uncertainty.

I knew what I was doing, and it had to happen this way. Denying us would be the end of me and now was the only time I could be with her. My feelings for her had been suppressed for years.

Kim opened her mouth and attempted to say something. I quickly put my finger over it. "Breathe," I told her. She inhaled deeply and exhaled repeatedly.

I kissed her while holding her hands over her head. I didn't need her to overthink this. Our kiss felt like forever. When I opened my eyes, tears were flowing from hers.

"Don't cry. It's okay. No one will know."

She grabbed my neck and pulled my head closer to her and kissed me. Our tongues were intertwined as I rubbed my hands around her waist and her hips. I wanted to feel every part of her body. I touched her hair and then took off her scrunchy. I wanted to see all of her. She tried to get up.

"What's wrong?" I asked. "Nothing and everything." I moved and let her sit up.

"Brian," she said, looking into my eyes. "We cannot do this."

"It's too late." I got on my knees in front of her and took her shirt off, revealing her breasts. She covered them with her arms and looked away.

"No, don't hide your body. I want to see you," I told her.

She looked down at her arms and I helped her pull them away. I leaned my head on her forehead while holding her hands with each of mine.

"You don't know how bad I want you right now," I whispered.

I grabbed her exposed thighs, spreading her legs to get even closer. We were face to face.

"Can I have you?" I asked.

Kim put her arms around my neck while looking down. When she looked up and into my eyes again, I had my answer. She pulled my shirt over my head. She rubbed my chest and kissed my neck, before kissing my lips. I felt her breasts on my skin and wanted her even more.

Every moment was higher than I had ever felt with anyone. She kept taking deep breaths. I backed away to look at her. I rubbed her breasts and she let out the sexiest moan. I kissed them slowly, taking her all in. My tongue met her skin and I licked a trail to her nipple. The sounds she let out made me take my time. I gave each breast equal attention and could tell she loved it.

Kim stood up, grabbed my hand, and walked me to her

bedroom. We stood in front of the bed kissing. I pushed my hand into her shorts rubbing all over her soft skin. I knew she felt me too. With her help, my pants dropped.

"Kim, we both know this can't happen again after tonight. I want all of you, don't hold back. You can be loud, scream, moan, whatever. Just let go and be with only me in this moment," I told her softly.

"Okay," she whispered.

I laid her down and pulled her shorts and panties off. She made sure I was as naked as she was. When I moved to lay down with her, she stopped me.

"No, stay there," she said.

My dick was pointing right at her. She sat up and faced it. Then she kissed it from the head to the base. When she got back to the tip, she put it in her mouth. I couldn't help but moan.

I wasn't expecting her to give me head, but it felt damn good. Anything she did would. I closed my eyes and held my head back enjoying every second. The faster she went, the louder I got. I pulled away when I was about to come.

"No holding back, right?" she asked with a sneaky smirk on her face.

Kim lay back on the bed pulling me onto her. We kissed again before she grabbed me.

"Put it in," she told me.

I followed her instruction. She was so wet, I almost let it go. I told her to give me a minute while still inside her. She kissed all over my face until I was ready again.

The night felt like it would never end. I put her in every position I knew of to make sure I felt her in every way possible. From the back she had me pull her hair, from the side she'd throw it back, then she got on top.

It was getting close to that point, I had to switch it up again. She screamed, I moaned, then we both let it all go. She came in almost every position and I was proud to have gotten her there each time. Her legs clamped around my waist the last time after I finished. It was more than I ever dreamed and enough to hold on to for a lifetime.

Kim went to the bathroom for a few minutes and came out with a towel for me to clean myself off. She got in the bed, facing me.

"That was amazing," she said. "Yeah, it was."

"Too bad it could never happen again."

"I know, but that's how it has to be."

"I understand."

She stared into my eyes until she turned around and backed up into me. I held her as we fell asleep.

CHAPTER
FOURTEEN

Kim

AFTER THIS WEEKEND, I KNEW THAT IT WAS TIME for me to move on with my life. Trent and I were definitely done, and it felt good to get over that hurdle of a relationship. I would never go back down that road again. My mom got an earful from my dad who attempted to make her apologize, but she didn't.

Then there was Brian. He made me believe in real love again. Even though I could never have it with him, I knew what it felt like and could identify it whenever it came my way. For as wrong of a thing we'd done, it was only right for me to distance myself from everyone. There was no way I could ever face him and be normal about it.

I had a long talk with Mrs. Roland at work and had decided to give my two-weeks' notice. As much as I loved my job, I hated my life outside of it more. I needed a fresh start somewhere that no one knew me.

Colorado was her solution for me, but it didn't feel like home when I was there. I didn't think I would enjoy living there long-term. In all the frustration and confusion my life had been lately, one thing was clear: I was leaving it all behind.

Aunt Vivica received the call she'd been waiting on from me. I let her know that I accepted the offer to move in with her until I figured out what I wanted to do. She screamed over the phone, running through all the things we'd do together and all the places she would take me around the world.

My poor aunt was lonely because her grown kids had their own families and lives. They couldn't pick up and go with her whenever she felt like it. I'd be that for her for as long as she needed. Everything else would come when it was time.

It was hard to confront my family about the decision, but it had to be done. I met all of them at a restaurant and told them the news. My dad was shocked since I don't usually do anything without a plan, but he told me he was proud that I was taking the time to find myself. Plus, he knew I'd be safe with his little sister. I was going to miss him more than anyone else.

I got everything in order for my move. It was scheduled for next month. I found a nice charity to donate all my furniture. Well, at least the things left after I gave my family first dibs. I began shipping my clothes and personal things to my aunt's house. A lot of my clothes were donated as well. I was going to start from scratch.

The plan was to take a year off from everything and then get back to it. I had no idea how I would afford living in California, well at least where I wanted to live. If I had peace, I could make anything work.

The last week before my one-way trip came, Sheryl paid me a visit. I explained to her that I was moving once she noticed my empty apartment. There was a pretty good seafood restaurant around the corner from my place that we went to for dinner.

"I can't believe you are leaving," she said, pouting.

"Yeah, it's time. There is nothing left for me here."

"Ugh, I'm here."

"Sheryl, you know what I mean. Besides, it would be weird hanging out with you and having to see your son with other people. Not that I want him back, but it's still not something I want to do."

"Trust me, I understand. You two have had a few ups and then nothing but downs."

We laughed. "Ain't that the truth."

"I tried my best with him. He still turned out to be like his dad. I will never understand how a child can turn out to be like a parent that was barely around. I guess he saw enough of him to be influenced."

"Hey, you did what you could like all good parents do. At a certain point, it's the child's turn to make their own decisions and there's nothing anyone can do about it. I had my share of screw-ups too, but I appreciate all of your support through it all."

"Always."

"I wish my mom was as supportive."

I told her about how my mom acted the last time we spoke. Sheryl was appalled. Even she apologized for my mother.

"People are who they are and how they are. I have learned after much resistance, that it is not my place to try and change anyone. I had to accept everyone as they were. It was my choice to either deal with them or walk away. So, my ass booked a flight."

She laughed. "I know that's right, girl."

We ate our dinner and talked about life. I never knew she went through a lot of the things I did. No wonder she always had my back. She knew firsthand what I was feeling.

I promised her that we would keep in touch. She was the type of woman I could really talk to and she listened. I needed more women in my life like that. After dinner, we said our final goodbye for a while.

ppp

MY DAD INVITED ME TO DINNER THE NIGHT BEFORE my flight. I told him it wasn't going to happen. I knew what he was up to and it was useless. He would see me tomorrow since he was supposed to drop me off at the airport.

Mom didn't want to accept my flaws. As hard as it was to understand, I couldn't change the past and didn't want the stress of trying to make her change.

I sat on my air mattress and watched TV on my phone for my last night in Houston. My show was interrupted by Trent's call. He was the last person I wanted to hear from. I never told him about me leaving and I planned to keep it that way. It was of no concern of his.

"Hello, Trenton."

"Why you gotta say my name like that?"

"Boy, what do you want?"

"I heard you were moving away for good." That damn Sheryl. "Yeah, I leave tomorrow."

"You weren't going to tell me?"

"I assumed you were busy with your hoes."

"Kim, I don't have hoes."

"That's not the word on the street. People hit me up asking what's wrong with you since they thought we were still together. It has happened multiple times.

So, don't lie. I don't care what you do anymore."

"Look, I didn't call to argue."

"I'm not. But you don't have to play dumb with me. I know what you've been doing."

"Well, can I see you?"

"For what?"

"To say goodbye."

"Trent, we can do that on the phone. Say it and I'll say it back. Then you can go back to the life you always wanted."

"You sound mad. I thought you didn't care."

"I don't. Now, can we say goodbye already." There was a knock at my door. "Hold on." I got up to answer it. Trent was there.

"Nope. Uh-uh."

"What?" he asked, laughing. "Don't even try it."

"Can I come in?"

"Sure, come in and sit on the floor."

He walked inside and looked around. "Damn, you are really leaving me."

"Nigga, please. You left me a long time ago."

"Ah, you still on that."

"Shut up. Why are you here?"

"I wanted to say goodbye in person. I mean damn. You were once my fiancée."

"Briefly."

Trent laughed. "Why are you even in this empty apartment? Shouldn't you be spending your last night with your family?"

"I would, but my mom never forgave me for getting pregnant."

"Damn. Hey, I'm sorry about all that. I had no idea your people didn't know about it."

"Yeah, well that's what I get for trying to keep a secret like that. Now, don't you have somewhere to be?"

"No, I cleared my night, so I could spend it with you."

"That was stupid. Why would you think I would want that?"

"So, you don't love me no more? That fast, you have no feelings for me?"

"Sorry, but no. Did you fall and hit your head or something? You do remember how we got here, right? Oh, yeah, I forgot you got knocked out recently."

"Ay, that shit ain't funny. I was caught off guard."

"Sure, you were."

"I don't suppose we could...you know?" He pulled me over to him.

"Hell, no. You might have herpes or some shit."

Trent laughed as I pushed him away. "So, you not going to miss it?"

"I haven't missed it so far."

"Why? You been messing with some other dude or something?"

"That's none of your business."

"Nah, if you were, you wouldn't be leaving. Unless he couldn't do it like me."

"Ha! Trust me, he was way better."

He backed away from me like he was trying to read me or something. "Yeah, right. You lying, right?"

"Anyway. I need to get some sleep if you don't mind."

"Oh, I can put you to sleep," he said, pulling at me again.

"No, thanks."

"For real?"

"For real, for real. I don't want your ass."

"Not even one last time."

"Nope."

"Damn. It's like that."

"It's exactly how you made it."

"A'ight then." Trent gave me a long hug and kissed my cheek. "I hope you have a good life and find someone that deserves you."

"You, too." We walked to the door.

"But you sure you don't want—"

"Get out, boy."

"Bye, Kimberly."

"Goodbye, Trenton."

I closed the door with Brian on the brain. The sooner I left, the better. A part of me wished it was him at the door.

♡♡♡

THE MORNING CAME, AND MY DAD WAS EARLY. He helped me get the rest of my things and we went to the car. My mom was sitting in the passenger seat. I stopped walking.

"Daddy," I whined.

"Now look, baby girl. You and your mother need to fix this mess before you leave. That's all there is to it."

"She's the one who hates me."

"You know she doesn't hate you. She wants the best for you."

We made our way to the car. I put on the best smile I could muster up. "Good morning, Mom."

"Good morning."

I sat in the back seat. She turned around. "You ready to leave us behind?"

"Mom, don't do that. What choice did I have? It's bad enough with everything I dealt with Trent. On top of it, my own mother basically rejected me for being human. So yes, I am ready to leave this life behind me."

"You think Vivica can give you a better one?"

"No. She is only helping out while *I* figure out what's better for me. That's all."

Mom turned back around, and Daddy started the car. I had him stop at the front office to drop off my keys and paperwork.

Most of the drive was quiet except for my phone that kept getting texts from people wishing me well. The closer we got, the more my dad tried to nudge my mom into apologizing. I told him that I didn't need it and he could stop. He did.

When we pulled up to the airport, we all got out of the car. Dad got my things from the trunk, which left me face to face with my mother.

"Well, I guess this is goodbye," she said. "It's not like you'll never see me again."

"It sure feels like it."

"I would never do that. Even though we fight, I love you. Nothing could make me never visit you."

"Oh, baby. Be careful, okay. You know that I love you too. I am sorry for what I said to you before."

An apology? I didn't think she had it in her. "Wow. That really means a lot."

We hugged, and Daddy handed me my things. He gave me a hug and a kiss, then I was on my way to California. It was bittersweet but more sweet than bitter. On to the next phase and a new life.

THE END...SORT OF (^o^)

I hope you enjoyed the story so far. If you're anything like me, you are pissed at these characters by now. As you have read, Kim and Brian just blew up their worlds with one selfish act. Find out what happens next. Continue to Making A Hard Right for a journey of self-love, self-discovery, and self-forgiveness. It's a roller coaster.

Also, your reviews matter. Feel free to write a review about book one in the Turns in Love series. Cuz these turns are hard ones LOL.

MAKING A HARD RIGHT EXCERPT

Kim

CHAPTER ONE

Since we had been back from Central and South America, my stomach had turned on me. Out of the blue, I woke up sick. In Mexico, I was so nauseous it ruined the end of our trip. Well, for me it did.

When I first arrived in Muir Beach, I was antsy. Back home, I had a perfectly good career that kept me busy, and now nothing. Moving here sounded marvelous in my mind. I planned to get over my relationship with Trent, my mom's constant "I'm so disappointed in you" breakdowns, and that one night of liquored-up dumb shit with Brian.

My cousins visited their mom with their families on my second night. It was a full house. Cory and Marissa had four kids aged seven and below. Malik and Tara only had two. They were preparing for a move into a new home closer to my aunt and Cory. Having the kids all together with their grandmother gave the exhausted parents a limited time to relax. I sat out on the balcony with the four of them while Aunt Vivica attempted to tame her grandchildren.

I learned that Marissa stayed at home with their four and Tara worked part-time at her boys' daycare. Since she worked with kids, she needed this quiet time more than anyone. I got along great with children, but I had no desire to spend my entire days drowning in them. My nephews back home were angels for a few hours with me. But if I kept them all day, every day, I'd lose it.

My cousins lived decent lives with beautiful families. When they found out I had recently broken off my engagement, the wheels turned in their heads. Married couples always wanted everyone else to tie the knot. The question came up about my plans regarding marriage and kids. I told them I'd be ready when the right guy came along to change my mind about it all.

For now, being single and having no little humans depending on me was for the best. Trent put a sour taste in my mouth when it came to long-term relationships. I didn't trust my judgment with men anymore.

With the first week of this new start under my belt, I needed to figure out how I'd use my time here. My aunt assured me I didn't need all the answers right away, but something had to occupy my days. Since this was a break from everything, I had to learn how to chill out.

Aunt Vivica jogged in the mornings, and she usually ran on the beach. The first time she woke me up, I dreaded going out there. Running and I did not mesh well. My feet never quite landed on the ground securely. At least that's what I thought when I tried in the past. My chest burned when I caught my breath. Maybe it was in my head, but I hated it either way.

This time proved me wrong. I had a purpose behind each step. We started off slow and before I knew it; we raced against each other daily. Aunt Vivica beat me in the beginning due to my rustiness. I became the champion by the fourth time. I didn't have a fitness motive, but a figurative one. I ran from Trent. I ran from Brian and Denise. And I ran toward my future.

After another two weeks, my aunt was ready to go somewhere, anywhere. Aunt Vivica didn't want to wait for me to settle in. She told me I had the rest of the year to do it. Instead, she scheduled a straight month of traveling. How could I say no to that? My empty passport needed stamps in this lifetime.

ᗐᗐᗐ

We began our journey to maximum relaxation for two and a half, peaceful weeks. She showed me a lifestyle I would work my ass off to get one day on my own. This trip gave me the motivation I never had before. The beaches appeared endless. The freshwater breeze flowed through our room, waking us up each morning. True paradise.

The first week, we visited Costa Rica at a resort off the beach called Occidental Papagayo. No kids allowed. Amen. I never saw a place more beautiful. The bright blue ocean blew my mind. I'd been accustomed to brown water shores in the Gulf of Mexico all my life.

My aunt was an outdoors person unlike me. I enjoyed the beach but not hiking, and long walks too close to nature. However, the trails and tours changed my heart. Some little creature had me jumping all over the place, but I loved it. Zip lining would also get a hell no any other time, but Aunt Vivica pushed me to let go and be free. I was glad I listened.

If anything changed me the most, it was the food. We ate the majority of our meals at the hotel, but a few times we ventured off and met the locals at nearby restaurants. Southern cuisine was the only thing I found pleasing to my palette. Until I had no other choice but to immerse myself into the different cultures and foods. It opened my eyes to a whole new world.

Buenos Aires, Argentina took the trip to another level. Alvear Palace Hotel provided a luxury I hadn't dreamed of experiencing. The place was straight out of a movie. Hell, for a few moments, I thought I hit the lotto. The gold accented decor and marble everywhere in our suite made me feel unworthy. The elegant dining and even more beautiful city were the highlights of my existence.

Our vacation traveled downhill in Mexico. My stomach had a mind of its own. The first thing I blamed was the food. I ate some of everything. Even though I enjoyed each bite, one of them turned on me. I didn't have the energy to do any of the activities I was eager to take part of. Aunt Viv kept me company, stating she didn't want to leave me alone. So, we lounged around in proximity to a bathroom for the last week of our trip.

Once we got back to California, nothing cured this bug. Aunt Vivica prepared homemade soups, which tasted great but didn't stay down. I kept myself hydrated and chilled on the balcony for fresh air as much as possible. By nighttime, the nausea died down and gave me hope that it passed. The next morning, I was once again on my knees in front of the toilet.

Days passed with no urge to do anything outside the house. I feared public humiliation if I couldn't get to a bathroom. So, we rented movies and ordered takeout. Marissa planned to come over with the kids, but I didn't want to get them sick. She'd have to handle her herd alone for one more week.

After another day of lying around doing nothing, I improved a little. We thought the worst had gone, so we went bowling. I threw up there too. My aunt worried that it was something serious and wanted to take me to the hospital. With the help of the internet, I self-diagnosed my symptoms as dehydration.

When I was still sick after a week, my aunt asked if I could be pregnant. I laughed it off. Trent and I never had unprotected sex after my miscarriage. Having his baby would have been a nail in the coffin. I made sure not to get caught up in that type of situation. Then the night with Brian came to mind. I didn't remember if we used a condom. There's no way we didn't. But does he even carry them?

The thought of him put me in the bathroom again. Life wouldn't be so cruel. What we did was supposed to stay hidden. If I was pregnant, I'd have to move to South America and never return. No one would look for me there.

Aunt Vivica bought three different tests at the local drugstore. A half hour later, all three confirmed the end of me. We sat in my room in silence. My aunt wiped away many tears from my face, but they wouldn't stop falling. Nothing mattered anymore. The very reason for my relocation was to rid myself of the past, old and recent, and go a different route. This one was way off course. I didn't know how I'd turn my life around with a baby that belonged to a married man.

Making a Hard Right is Available Now!

ABOUT THE AUTHOR

Renée is from the best city on the planet—Houston. She resides there with her three kids. She writes fiction based on African American characters. Renée loves creating stories with relationship drama that can easily be found in many households. She wants readers to see themselves or recognize someone they know in her characters. If she can make you laugh, gasp, think, or even cry, then her mission will be accomplished.

Connect with Renée: www.authorramoses.com
    On Facebook www.facebook.com/authorramoses
    On Instagram @reneeamoses
    On Twitter @authorramoses

Listen to Same Book, 3 Time Zones: A Book Review Podcast
    We read one book a month and post our discussion.
    www.sb3tzreviews.com
    On Instagram @sb3tz_reviews

Signup for latest news, first looks, and exclusive content: bit.ly/RAMList

ALSO BY RENÉE A. MOSES

Turns in Love Series

*Two Lefts, One Right**

Making a Hard Right

Straightaway

Wishing for Her (Christmas Short)

Truth Is...

Harris Sisters Series

The Cost of Loving You

I Thought I Knew You

Never Stopped Loving You

Not Good Enough For You

Standalone

You Could Do Damage

When the Time is Wright (Christmas Novella)